SEBASTOPOL

SEBASTOPOL
by Leo Tolstoi

Introduction by Philip Rahv

ANN ARBOR PAPERBACKS

THE UNIVERSITY OF MICHIGAN PRESS

First edition as an Ann Arbor Paperback 1961
Introduction copyright © by The University of Michigan 1961
All rights reserved
Published in the United States of America by
The University of Michigan Press and simultaneously
in Toronto, Canada, by Ambassador Books Limited
Translated by Frank D. Millet
Manufactured in the United States of America

INTRODUCTION By Philip Rahv

THE CRIMEAN WAR of 1854-56, of which
Tolstoi's *Sebastopol* constitutes an un-
equaled record, was chiefly caused by the
aggressive policies of Tsar Nicholas I, that
most autocratic of all autocrats, in further-
ing the perennial Russian drive toward the
Balkans and the Bosporus. The response
of the vigilant Western powers, England
and France primarily, was to resort to
arms in defense of what they considered
their vital strategic interests to be at that
time, though it goes without saying that
they chose to present their cause to world
opinion as an heroic struggle of "civiliza-
tion against barbarism." The most flag-
rant errors of military judgment and execution were perpetrated both by the
Russians and the Allies. The losses were
consequently enormous; it is estimated
that in the siege of Sebastopol the Russian
army alone lost somewhat more than

100,000 men in killed and wounded, while the total casualties of all the belligerents reached the figure of 600,000. The principal result of the Crimean War was the shattering of the then prevailing myth of the invincibility of Russian arms and the exposure of the administrative and socio-economic backwardness of the Russian empire. It was a disastrous war for imperial Russia, and its effect was to convince even some of the most conservative circles of the Russian upper strata that the petrified society over which Nicholas had presided with such self-complacent brutality had no future and that fundamental reforms had become inevitable. The most far-reaching of those reforms was, of course, the abolition of serfdom in 1861.

Tolstoi was in his twenty-fifth year when he joined the besieged garrison of Sebastopol in November 1854. He was then by no means a novice in the art of war, for he had previously served with distinction for several years as a *junker* attached to an artillery unit in the Cossack country on the Terek. (The rich and varied experience of that period later found its admirable creative embodiment in such long stories as *The Cossacks* and the posthumously published *Hadji Murad*, one of the very finest of his narratives and perhaps one of the least known of Tolstoi's works among English-speaking readers.) In 1854 he received his commission and volunteered for active service in the army then fighting the Turks in Wallachia. As the Crimean War gathered force and the Russians retreated from the Danubian provinces, Tolstoi was transferred at his own request to Sebastopol. In those late months of 1854 he was no doubt under the sway of the patriotic enthusiasm that swept the nation at the news of the epic struggle which the Sebastopol garrison was conducting against the invaders despite initial routs and defeats. His mood of patriotic exaltation may be gauged from his letter to his brother Sergei written but a few days after his arrival at the naval base: "The spirit among the troops is beyond description. In the time of ancient Greece there was not so much heroism. Admiral Kornilov, making the round of his troops, instead of hailing them with: 'Good health to you, lads!'

says: 'If you must die, lads, will you die?'
And the soldiers shout: 'We will die, Your
Excellency, Hurrah!' And they do not say
it for effect, for in every face one saw not
jesting but earnestness, and 22,000 men
have already fulfilled that promise." Tolstoi stayed in Sebastopol till the end of
October 1855, and he fought in the battle
of the Chernaya as well as at the famous
Fourth Bastion, the most dangerously exposed position in the maze of Russian
earthworks, where he was stationed for a
time in command of a battery.

But Tolstoi's mood of patriotic exaltation lasted but a few months, as can be seen
from the difference between the first of the
tales, "Sebastopol in December, 1854,"
and the tales that follow it. In the first tale
he observes the faces, the bearing and the
movement of the troops, and what is
visible to him above all are those "chief
traits" constituting "the power of Russia—
simplicity and straightforwardness . . ." He
is convinced that the horrors of war have
produced in the combatants the consciousness of personal worth, emotion, and lofty
thought; and he is equally positive that the

Introduction

Russian men are fighting not for medals, titles, or because of threats; the nobler incentive that animates them is "love of country." No wonder legend has it that Alexander II, the successor of Nicholas, was so affected by this tale that he ordered it translated into French and counseled his commanders at Sebastopol "to take care of the life of that young man." All is different, however, in the next tale, "Sebastopol in May, 1855." Of idealized patriotism there is virtually no trace left. The stress is no longer on "love of country" but on something altogether different that belongs to the author alone: "The hero of my tale, whom I love with all the strength of my soul . . . is the truth." Thus, here the representation of men at war acquires the typical Tolstoyan edge and originality, breaking through conventional modes of perception toward the analysis of the process of feeling in its minute changes and transmutations. A new note of realism is struck in the portrayal of officers like Kalouguine and his comrades, who are now seen as plainly actuated by vanity, the desire to shine, and the hope of reward

and reputation. Men are evaluated for
what they are and war for what it is.
Tolstoi's Christian conscience is outraged
by the insensate slaughter he has wit-
nessed, and he barely avoids outright con-
demnation of the war by the thought,
which at any rate gives him but small comfort, that it is not the Russians who ini-
tiated it—"we are only defending our own
country, our fatherland."

It therefore comes as no surprise to
learn that the editors of the magazine *The
Contemporary*, in which these tales were
printed, had a great deal of trouble getting
"Sebastopol in May" through the censor-
ship. In fact it did not escape mutilation
at the hands of the authorities, who charged
the author with "ridiculing our brave
officers." Nekrasov, one of the editors of
the magazine, wrote to Tolstoi in Septem-
ber 1855: "The revolting mutilation of
your tale quite upset me. Even now I cannot think of it without regret or rage.
Your work will, of course, not be lost . . . it
will remain as proof of a strength able to
utter such profound and sober truth under
circumstances amid which few men would

have retained it. It is just what Russian
society now needs: the truth—the truth,
of which since Gogol's death so little has
remained in Russian literature." And during the same month Tolstoi notes in his
Diary: "Yesterday I received news that
"Sebastopol in May" has been distorted
and printed. It seems that I am under the
strict observation of the Blues [the gen-
darmes] on account of my writings. . . ." So
much for telling the truth in wartime.

But apart from the ethical content of
these tales, such as the tendency toward
Christian pacifism by which Tolstoi was
completely ruled in later life, what is of
further interest is his approach to war as a
literary theme specifically—an approach
which, directly or indirectly, has greatly
influenced all subsequent writers on war
including such Americans as Stephen Crane
and Ernest Hemingway. What must be
noted above all is that already in these
early narratives Tolstoi has characteristi-
cally renounced the heroic and romantic
conventions with which this theme had
been traditionally associated, concentrat-
ing instead on the depiction of war in terms

faithful to the actual experience of men under fire, an experience singularly bewildering and singularly incoherent. In this respect he is, of course, indebted to Stendhal, whom he openly acknowledged as his master in military realism. Thus, he once spoke to Paul Boyer of Stendhal as having taught him to understand war. "Re-read," he said to him, "the description of the battle of Waterloo in *La Chartreuse de Parme*. Whoever before has so described war? Described it, that is, as it is in reality? Do you remember Fabrice riding over the field of battle and understanding 'nothing'?" Yet Tolstoi proceeded much further than Stendhal in breaking down the stereotypes that beset writers on war, for he was able to represent the fear and courage manifested by men in battle not primarily as individual traits given once and for all but as involuntary sensations all the more terrifying because of their unexpectedness and extremity.

The eleven months that Tolstoi spent in Sebastopol were not entirely absorbed by military life. He was able to keep up his Diary, in which we find any number

of entries quite detached from his immed-
iate experiences. Of particular and sur-
passing interest is the following notation
of March 5, 1855:

"A conversation about Divinity and
Faith has suggested to me a great, a stu-
pendous idea, to the realization of which I
feel capable of devoting my life. That idea
is the founding of a new religion corres-
ponding to the present state of mankind:
the religion of Christ but purged of dogmas
and mysticism—a practical religion, not
promising future bliss but giving bliss on
earth. I understand that to accomplish
this the conscious labor of generations will
be needed. One generation will bequeath the
idea to the next, and some day fanaticism
or reason will accomplish it. *Deliberately* to
promote the union of mankind by religion
is the basic thought which I hope will
dominate me."

This programmatic statement, so as-
tounding in its prodigious sweep and audac-
ity, clearly anticipates that which Tolstoi
endeavored to achieve in later life, in the
period of unrest and religious crisis that
opens with his writing of *My Confession*

and his renunciation of the joys of the natural world. But in between came the years of overwhelming commitment to his narrative art, the incomparable years of *Anna Karenina* and *War and Peace*. Not that he ever wholly forgot the idea of founding a "practical religion not promising future bliss but giving bliss on earth," for there are distinct preoccupations in both great novels that show the permanent hold this idea had on him.

What Tolstoi saw and felt as an officer in the Sebastopol garrison proved to be of immense value both in the way in which it helped him to acquire the capacity to depict war with unexampled realism and in the way in which it contributed to the shaping of his sensibility in its revulsion against all those actions of men that serve to deny the Christian principle of love and brotherhood.

SEBASTOPOL IN DECEMBER, 1854

SEBASTOPOL.

SEBASTOPOL IN DECEMBER, 1854.

DAWN tinges the horizon above Mount Sapouné; the shadows of the night have left the surface of the sea, which, now dark blue in color, only awaits the first ray of sunshine to sparkle merrily; a cold wind blows from the fog-enveloped bay; there is no snow on the ground, the earth is black, but frost stings the face and cracks underfoot. The quiet of the morning is disturbed only by the incessant murmuring of the waves, and is broken at long intervals by the dull roar of cannon. All is silent on the men-of-war; the hour-glass has just marked the eighth hour. Towards the north the activity of day replaces little by little the tranquillity of night. On this side a detachment of soldiers is going to relieve the guard, and the click of their guns can be heard; a surgeon hurries towards his hospital; a soldier crawls out of his hut, washes his sunburned face with icy water, turns towards the east, and repeats a prayer, making rapid signs of the cross. On that side an enormous, heavy cart with creaking wheels reaches the cemetery where they are going to bury the corpses heaped almost to the top of the vehicle. Approach the harbor and you are disagreeably surprised by a mixture of odors; you smell coal, manure, moisture, meat. There are thousands of different objects: wood, flour, gabions, beef, thrown in heaps here and there; soldiers of different regiments, some provided with guns and with bags, others with neither guns nor bags, crowd together; they smoke, they quarrel, and they bear loads upon the steamer stationed near the plank bridge and ready to sail. Small private boats, filled with all sorts of people —soldiers, sailors, merchants, and women— are constantly arriving and departing. " This way for Grafskaya!" and two or three retired sailors rise in their boats and offer you their services. You choose the nearest one, stride over the half-decomposed body of a black horse lying in the mud two steps from

the boat, and seat yourself near the helm.
You push off from the shore ; all around
you the sea sparkles in the morning sun ; in
front of you an old sailor in an overcoat of
camel's-hair cloth and a lad with blond hair
are diligently rowing. You turn your eyes
upon the gigantic ships with scratched hulls
scattered over the harbor, upon the shallops,
—black dots on the sparkling azure of the
water—upon the pretty houses of the town,
to whose light-colored tones the rising sun
gives a rosy tinge, upon the hostile fleet
standing like light-houses in the crystalline
distance of the sea, and, at last, upon the
foaming waves, where play the salt drops
which the oars dash into the air. You
hear at the same time the regular sound of
voices which comes over the water, and the
grand roar of the cannonade at Sebastopol,
which seems to increase in strength as you
listen.

At the thought that you, you also, are in
Sebastopol, your whole soul is filled with a
sentiment of pride and of valor, and your
blood runs quicker in your veins.

"Straight towards the *Constantine*, your
excellency," says the old sailor, turning

around to the direction you are giving to the helm.

"Look! she has still got all her cannons," remarks the lad with the blond hair as the boat glides along the side of the ship.

"She is quite new, she ought to have them. Korniloff lives on board," repeats the old man, examining in his turn the man-of-war.

"There! it has burst!" cries the lad, after a long silence, his eyes fixed upon a small white cloud of drifting smoke suddenly appearing in the sky above the south bay, and accompanied by the strident noise of a shell explosion.

"They are firing from the new battery to-day," adds the sailor, calmly spitting in his hand. "Come along, Nichka; pull away. Let's pass the shallop."

And the small boat moves rapidly over the undulating surface of the bay, leaves the heavy shallop behind laden with bags and with soldiers, unskilful rowers who are pulling awkwardly, and at last lands in the middle of a great number of boats moored to the shore in the harbor of Grafskaya. A crowd of soldiers in gray overcoats, sailors in black jackets, and women in motley gowns comes and goes on the quay. Some peasants are selling bread; others, seated beside their samovars, offer to customers warm drink.

Here, on the upper steps of the landing, are strewn about, pell-mell, rusty shot, shell, canister, cast-iron cannon of different calibres; there, farther away, in a great open square, are lying enormous joists, gun-carriages, sleeping soldiers. On one side are wagons, horses, cannon, artillery caissons, stacks of muskets; farther on, soldiers, sailors, officers, women, and children are moving about; carts full of bread, bags, and barrels, a Cossack on horseback, a general in his droschky, are crossing the square. A barricade looms up in the street to the right, and in its embrasures are small cannon, beside which a sailor is sitting quietly smoking his pipe. On the left stands a pretty house, on the pediment of which are scrawled numerals, and above can be seen soldiers and blood-stained stretchers. The dismal traces of a camp in war-time meet the eye everywhere. Your first impression is, doubtless, a disagreeable one; the strange amal-

gamation of town life with camp life, of an
elegant city and a dirty bivouac, strikes you
like a hideous incongruity. It seems to you
that all, overcome by terror, are acting vac-
uously; but if you examine the faces of those
men who are moving about you, you will
think differently. Look well at this soldier
of the wagon-train who is leading his bay
troitka horses to drink, humming through
his teeth, and you shall find that he does not
go astray in this confused crowd, which in
fact does not exist for him, for he is full of
his own business, and will do his duty, whatever it is—will lead his horses to the water-
ing - place or drag a cannon with as much
calm and assured indifference as if he were
at Toula or at Saransk. You notice the
same expression on the face of this officer,
with his irreproachable white gloves, who is
passing before you, of that sailor who sits on
the barricade smoking, of the soldiers who
wait with their stretchers at the door of
what was lately the Assembly Hall, even
upon the face of the young girl who crosses
the street, leaping from stone to stone for
fear of soiling her pink dress. Yes, a great
deception awaits you on your arrival at Se-

bastopol. In vain you seek to discover upon any face traces of agitation, fright, indeed even enthusiasm, resignation to death, resolution; there is nothing of all that. You see the course of every-day life; see people occupied with their daily toils, so that, in fact, you blame yourself for your exaggerated exaltation, and doubt not only the truth of the opinion you have formed from hearsay about the heroism of the defenders of Sebastopol, but also doubt the accuracy of the description which has been given you on the north side and the sinister sounds which fill the air there. Before doubting, however, go up to a bastion, see the defenders of Sebastopol on the very place of the defence, or rather enter straight into this house at whose door stand the stretcher-bearers. You will see there the heroes of the army, you will see there horrible and heart-rending sights, both sublime and comic, but wonderful and of a soul-elevating nature. Enter this great hall, which before the war was the hall of the Assembly. Scarcely have you opened the door before the odor exhaled from forty or fifty amputations and severe wounds turns you sick. You must not yield to the feeling which keeps you on the threshold of the room, it is an unworthy feeling; go boldly in, and not blush at having come to look at these martyrs. You may approach and speak with them. The wretches like to see a pitying face, to relate their sufferings, and to hear words of charity and sympathy. Passing down the middle between the beds, you look for the face which is the least rigid, the least contracted by pain, and on finding it decide to go near and put a question.

"Where are you wounded?" you hesitatingly ask an old, emaciated soldier, seated on his bed, watching you with a kindly look, and apparently inviting you to approach. You have, I say, put this question hesitatingly, because the sight of the sufferer inspires not only a lively pity, but also a sort of dread of hurting his feelings, joined with a profound respect.

"On the foot," replies the soldier; and nevertheless you notice by the folds of the blanket that his leg has been cut off above the knee.

"God be praised!" he adds, "I shall be discharged."

"Were you wounded long since?"

"It is the sixth week, your excellency."

"Where do you feel badly now?"

"Nowhere only in my calf when it is bad weather; nothing but that."

"How did it happen?"

"On the fifth bastion, your excellency, in the first bombardment. I had just sighted the cannon, and was going quietly to the other embrasure, when suddenly something struck my foot. I thought I had fallen into a hole. I looked—my leg was gone!"

"You didn't have any pain at first, then?"

"None at all, only just as if I had scald-ed my leg; that's all."

"And afterwards?"

"None afterwards, only when they stretch-ed the skin; that was a little rough. First of all things, your excellency, we mustn't think. When we don't think we don't feel. When a man thinks, it is the worse for him."

Meanwhile, a woman dressed in gray, with a black kerchief tied around her head, ap-proaches, joins in the conversation, and be-gins to give a detailed account of the sailor: how he has suffered, how his life was de-

spaired of for four weeks, how, when wounded, he made them stop the stretcher on which
he was being carried to the rear in order to
watch the discharge of our battery, and how
the grand-dukes had spoken with him, had
given him twenty - five rubles, and how he
had replied that, not being able to serve any
more himself, he would like to come back to
the bastion to train the conscripts. The
good woman, her eyes sparkling with enthusiasm, relates this in one breath, looking
at you and then at the sailor, who turns
away and pretends not to hear, busy with
picking lint from his pillow.

" It is my wife, your excellency," says the
sailor at last, with an intonation of voice
which seems to say, " You must excuse her;
all that is woman's foolish prattle, you
know."

You then begin to understand what the
defenders of Sebastopol are, and you are
ashamed of yourself in the presence of this
man. You would have liked to express all
your admiration for him, all your sympathy,
but the words will not come, or those which
do come are worthless, and you can only
bow in silence before this unconscious gran-

deur, before this firmness of soul and this exquisite shame of his own merit.

"Ah, well, may God speedily cure you!" you say, and you stop before another wounded man lying on the floor, who, suffering horrible pain, seems to be awaiting his death. He is blond, and his pale face is much swollen. Stretched on his back, his left hand thrown up, his position indicates acute suffering. His hissing breath escapes with difficulty from his dry, half-open mouth. The glassy blue pupils of his eyes are rolled up under the eyelids, and a mutilated arm, wrapped in bandages, sticks out from under the tumbled blanket. A nauseating, corpse-like odor rises to your nostrils, and the fever which burns the sufferer's limbs seems to penetrate your own body.

"Is he unconscious?" you ask of the woman who kindly accompanies you, and to whom you are no longer a stranger.

"No; he can still hear, but he is very bad;" and she adds, under her breath, "I have just made him drink a little tea. He is nothing to me, only I have pity on him; indeed, he has only been able to swallow a few mouthfuls."

" How do you feel?" you ask him.

At the sound of your voice the wounded man's eyes turn towards you, but he neither sees nor understands.

" That burns my heart !" he murmurs.

A little farther on an old soldier is changing his clothes. His face and his body are both of the same brown color, and as thin as a skeleton. One of his arms has been amputated at the shoulder. He is seated on his bed, he is out of danger, but from his dull, lifeless look, from his frightful thinness, from his wrinkled face, you see that this creature has already passed the greater part of his existence in suffering.

On the opposite bed you see the pale, delicate, pain-shrivelled face of a woman whose cheeks are flushed with fever.

" It is a sailor's wife. A shell hit her on the foot while she was carrying dinner to her husband in the bastion," says the guide.

" Has it been amputated ?"

" Above the knee."

Now, if your nerves are strong, enter there at the left. It is the operating-room. There you see surgeons with pale and serious countenances, their arms blood - splashed to the elbows, beside the bed of a wounded man, who, stretched on his back with open eyes, is delirious under the influence of chloroform, and utters broken phrases, some unimportant, some touching. The surgeons are busy with their repulsive but beneficent task, amputation. You see the curved and keen blade penetrate the healthy white flesh. The wounded man suddenly comes to himself with heart-rending cries, with curses. The assistant surgeon throws the arm into a corner, while another wounded man on a stretcher who sees the operation turns and groans, more on account of the mental torture of expectation than from the physical pain he feels. You will witness these horrible, heart-rending scenes; you will see war without the brilliant and accurate alignment of troops, without music, without the drum-roll, without standards flying in the wind, without galloping generals—you will see it as it is, in blood, in suffering, and in death! Leaving this house of pain, you will experience a certain impression of well-being, you will take long breaths of fresh air, and will be glad to feel yourself in good health; but at the same time the contemplation of these

misfortunes will have convinced you of your
own insignificance, and you will go up into
a bastion without hesitation. What are the
sufferings and the death of an atom like me,
you will ask yourself, in comparison with
these innumerable sufferings and deaths?
Besides, in a short time the sight of the pure
sky, of the bright sun, of the pretty city, of
the open church, of the soldiers coming and
going in all directions, raises your spirits to
their normal state. Habitual indifference,
preoccupation with the present and with its
petty interests, resume the ascendant. Perhaps you will meet on your way the funeral
cortége of an officer—a red coffin followed
by a band and by unfurled standards—and
perhaps the roar of the cannonade on the
bastion will strike your ear, but your thoughts
of a few moments before will not come back
again. The funeral will only be a pretty
picture for you, the growl of the cannon a
grand military accompaniment, and there
will be nothing in common between this
picture, these sounds, and the clear, personal impression of suffering and death called
up by the sight of the operating-room.

Pass the church, the barricade, and you

enter the most animated, the liveliest quar-
ter of the city. On both sides of the street
are shop signs, eating-house signs. Here
are merchants, women with men's hats or
with handkerchiefs on their heads, officers
in elegant uniforms. Everything testifies to
the courage, the assurance, the safety of the
inhabitants.

Enter this restaurant on the right. If
you want to listen to the sailors' and the
officers' talk, you will hear them relate the
incidents of the night before, of the affair
of the 24th; hear them grumble at the high
price of the badly cooked cutlets, and men-
tion the comrade recently killed.

" Devil take me! we are badly off where
we are now," says the bass voice of a pale,
blond, beardless, newly appointed officer, his
neck wrapped in a green knit scarf.

" Where is that?" some one asks.

" In the fourth bastion," replies the young
officer; and at this reply you attentively
look at him, and feel a certain respect for
him. His exaggerated carelessness, his violent gestures, his too loud laughter, which
would shortly before have seemed to you
impudent, become in your eyes the index of

a certain kind of combative spirit common to all young people who are exposed to great danger, and you are sure he is going to explain that it is on account of the shells and the bullets that they are so badly off in the fourth bastion. Nothing of the kind! They are badly off there because the mud is deep.

"Impossible to get up to the battery," he says, pointing to his boots, muddied even to the upper-leathers.

"My best gun captain was instantly killed to-day by a ball in his forehead," rejoins a comrade.

"Who was it? Mituchine?"

"No, another man.—Look here! are you never going to bring me my chop, you villain?" says he, speaking to the waiter.—"It was Abrossinoff, as brave a man as lived. He took part in six sorties."

At the other end of the table two infantry officers are eating veal cutlets with green pease washed down by sour Crimean wine, by courtesy called Bordeaux. One of them, a young man with red collar and two stars on his coat, is telling to his neighbor with a black collar and no stars the details of the

fight on the Alma. The first is a little the
worse for liquor. His frequently interrupted tale, his uncertain look, which reflects the
lack of confidence which his story inspires
in his auditor, the fine part he gives himself,
the too high color of his picture, lead you
to guess that he is wandering away from
the absolute truth. But you haven't anything to do with these tales, which you will
hear for a long time yet in the farthest corners of Russia; you have one wish alone,
that is, to go straight to the fourth bastion,
which you have heard so many and so varied reports about. You will notice that
whoever tells you he has been there says it
with pride and satisfaction; that whoever is
getting ready to go there either shows a little emotion or affects an exaggerated *sang-
froid*. If one man is joking with another,
he will invariably tell him, "Go to the fourth
bastion !" If a wounded man on a stretcher
is met, and he is asked where he comes from,
he will answer, almost without fail, " From
the fourth bastion !" Two completely different notions of this terrible earthwork have
been circulated; the first by those who have
never put their foot upon it, and for whom

it is the inevitable tomb of its defenders, the
second by those who, like the little blond
officer, live there and simply speak of it, saying it is dry or muddy there, warm or cold.

During the half hour you have been in the
restaurant the weather has changed and the
fog which spread over the sea has risen.
Thick, gray, moist clouds hide the sun.
The sky is gloomy, and a fine rain mixed
with snow is falling, wetting the roofs, the
sidewalks, and the soldiers' overcoats. After
passing one more barricade you go along up
the broad street. There are no more shop-
signs; the houses are uninhabitable, the
doors fastened up with boards, the windows
broken. On this side the corner of a wall
has been carried away, on that side the roof
has been broken in. The buildings look
like old veterans tried by grief and misery, and stare at you with pride, one might
say with disdain even. On the way you
stumble over cannon-balls and into holes,
filled with water, which the shells have made
in the rocky ground. You pass detach-
ments of soldiers and officers. You occasionally meet a woman or a child, but here
the woman does not wear a hat. As for the

sailor's wife, she wears an old fur cloak, and has soldiers' boots on her feet. The street now leads down a gentle declivity, but there are no more houses around you, nothing but shapeless masses of stones, of boards, of beams, and of clay. Before you, on a steep hill, stretches a black space, all muddy, and cut up with ditches. What you are looking at is the fourth bastion.

Passers become rare, no more women are met. The soldiers walk with rapid step. A few drops of blood stain the path, and you see coming towards you four soldiers bearing a stretcher, and on the stretcher a face of a sallow paleness and a bloody coat. If you ask the bearers where he is wounded, they will reply, with an irritated tone, without looking at you, that he has been hit on the arm or on the leg. If his head has been carried away, if he is dead, they will keep a morose silence.

The near whiz of balls and shells gives you a disagreeable impression while you are climbing the hill, and suddenly you have an entirely different idea from the one you recently had of the meaning of the cannon-shots heard in the city. I do not know

what placid and sweet souvenir will suddenly shine out in your memory. Your intimate
ego will occupy you so actively that you will
no longer think of noticing your surroundings. You will permit yourself to be overcome by a painful feeling of irresolution.
However, the sight of a soldier who, with
extended arms, is slipping down the hill in
the liquid mud, and passes near you, running
and laughing, silences your small inward
voice, the cowardly counsellor which arises
in you in the presence of danger. You
straighten up in spite of yourself, you raise
your head, and you, in your turn, scale the
slippery slope of the clay hill. You have
scarcely gone a step before musket-balls
hum in your ears, and you ask yourself if it
would not be preferable to go under côver
of the trench thrown up parallel with the
path. But the trench is full of a yellow,
fetid, liquid mud, so that you are obliged to
go on in the path; all the more since it is
the way everybody goes. At the end of
two hundred paces you come out on a place
surrounded by gabions, embankments, shelters, platforms supporting enormous cast-
iron cannon, and heaps of symmetrically

piled cannon-balls. These heaps of things give you the impression of a strange and aimless disorder. Here on the battery assembles a group of sailors; there in the middle of the enclosure lies a dismounted cannon, half buried in the sticky mud, through which an infantryman, musket in hand, is going to the battery, pulling out with difficulty first one foot and then the other. Everywhere in this liquid mud you see broken glass, unexploded shells, cannon - balls — every trace of camp life. You seem to hear the noise of a cannon-ball falling only two yards away, and from all sides come the sound of balls, which sometimes hum like bees, sometimes groan and split the air, which vibrates like a violin-string, the whole dominated by the sinister rumbling of cannon, which shakes you from head to foot and fills you with terror.

This is, then, the fourth bastion, this really terrible place, you say to yourself, feeling a little pride and a great deal of repressed fear. Not at all! You are the sport of an illusion. This is not yet the fourth bastion; it is the Jason redoubt, a place which, comparatively, is neither dangerous nor frightful. In order to reach the fourth bastion you enter the narrow trench which the infantryman follows, stooping over. You will perhaps see more stretchers, sailors, soldiers with spades, wires leading to the mines, earth-shelters equally muddy, into which only two men can crawl, and where the battalions of the Black Sea Sharpshooters live, eat, smoke, and put their boots on and off, in the midst of the débris of cast-iron of every form thrown here and there. You will perhaps find here four or five sailors playing cards in the shelter of the parapet, and a naval officer, who, seeing a new face come up, and a spectator at that, will be really pleased to initiate you into the details of the arrangements and give you an explanation of them. This officer, seated on a cannon, is rolling a cigarette with such coolness, passes so quietly from one embrasure to another, and talks with you with such natural calmness, that you recover your own *sang-froid*, in spite of the balls which are whistling here in greater numbers. You ask him questions, and even listen to his tales. The sailor will describe to you, if you will only ask him, the bombardment of the 5th, the

state of his battery with a single serviceable
cannon, his men reduced to eight, and, moreover, on the morning of the 6th, the battery
fired with every gun.   He will tell you also
how, on the 5th, a shell penetrated a bomb-
proof and struck down eleven sailors.   He
will show you, through the embrasure, the
enemy's trenches and batteries, which are
only thirty or forty fathoms distant.   I fear,
however, that, leaning out of the embrasure
in order to examine the enemy better, you
will see nothing, or that, if you perceive
something, you will be very much surprised
to learn that this white and rocky rampart
a few steps away, and from which are spout-
ing little clouds of smoke, is really the enemy—"*him*," as the soldiers and sailors
say.

It is very possible that the officer, either
through vanity or simply, without reflection,
to amuse himself, will be willing to have
them fire for you.   At his order the captain
of the gun and the men, fourteen sailors all
told, gayly approach the cannon to load it,
some chewing biscuit, others cramming their
short pipes in their pockets, while their hob-
nailed shoes clatter on the platform.   No-

tice the faces of these men, their bearing,
their movements, and you will recognize in
each of the wrinkles of their sunburned faces
with high cheek-bones, in each muscle, in
the breadth of the shoulders, in the thickness of the feet shod with colossal boots, in
each calm and bold gesture, the principal
elements that make up the strength of Russia — simplicity and obstinacy. You will
also see that danger, misery, and suffering
in the war will have imprinted on these
faces the consciousness of their dignity, of
high thoughts, of a sentiment.

Suddenly a deafening noise makes you
quake from head to foot. You hear at the
same instant the shot whistling away, while
a thick powder-smoke envelops the platform
and the black figures of sailors moving
about. Listen to their conversation, notice
their animation, and you will discover among
them a feeling which you would not expect
to meet—that of hatred of the enemy, of
vengeance. " It fell straight into the embrasure; two killed. Look! they are carrying them away," and they shout for joy.
" But he is getting angry now, he is going
to hit back," says a voice, and in truth you

see at the same instant a flash and spurting smoke, and the sentinel on the parapet calls, " Cannon !" A ball whizzes in your ears and buries itself in the ground, digging it up and casting around a shower of earth and stones. The commander of the battery gets angry, renews the order to load a second, a third gun. The enemy replies, and you experience interesting sensations. The sentinel again calls, "Cannon !" and the same sound, the same blow, and the same throwing up of earth are repeated. If, on the other hand, he cries, " Mortar !" you will be struck by a regular, not disagreeable hissing, which has no connection in your mind with anything terrible. It comes nearer and with greater rapidity. You see the black ball fall to the ground, and the bomb-shell burst with a metallic cracking. The pieces fly in air, whistling and screeching; stones hit each other, and mud splashes over you. You feel a strange mixture of pleasure and fright at these different sounds. At the instant the projectile reaches you, you invariably think it will kill you. But pride keeps you up, and no one notices the dagger that is digging into your heart. So

when it has passed without grazing you,
you live again; for an instant a feeling of
indescribable sweetness possesses you to
such a degree that you find a special charm
in danger, in the game of life and death.
You would like to have a ball or a shell fall
nearer, very near you.   But the sentinel an-
nounces with his strong, full voice, "Mortar!"   The hissing, the blow, the explosion
are repeated, but accompanied this time by
a human groan.   You go up to the wounded man at the same time with the stretcher-
bearers.   He has a strange look, lying in
the mud mingled with his blood.   Part of
his chest has been carried away.   In the
first moment his mud-splashed face express-
es only fright and the premature sensation
of pain, a feeling familiar to man in this situation.   But when they bring the stretcher
to him, and he unassisted lies down on it on
his uninjured side, an exalted expression,
elevated but restrained thoughts, enliven his
features.   With brilliant eyes and shut teeth
he raises his head with an effort, and at the
moment the stretcher-bearers move he stops
them, and addressing his comrades with
trembling voice, says, "Good-by, brothers!"

He would like to say something more, he
seems to be trying to find something touching to say, but he limits himself to repeating, " Good-by, brothers !" A comrade ap-
proaches the wounded man, puts his cap on
his head for him, and turns back to his cannon with a gesture of perfect indifference.
At the sight of your terrified expression of
face the officer, yawning, and rolling between
his fingers a cigarette in yellow paper, says,
" So it is every day, up to seven or eight
men."

You have just seen the defenders of Sebastopol on the very place of the defence,
and, strange to say, you will retrace your
steps without paying the least attention to
the bullets and balls which continue to whistle the whole length of the road as far as
the ruins of the theatre. You walk with
calmness, your soul elevated and strength-
ened, for you bring away the consoling conviction that never, and in no place, can the
strength of the Russian people be broken ;
and you have gained this conviction not
from the solidity of the parapets, from the in-
geniously combined intrenchments, from the
number of mines, from the cannon heaped

one on the other, and all of which you
have not in the least understood, but from
the eyes, the words, the bearing, from what
may be called the spirit of the defenders of
Sebastopol.

There is so much simplicity and so little
effort in what they do that you are per-
suaded that they could, if it were necessary,
do a hundred times more, that they could
do everything. You judge that the sentiment that impels them is not the one you
have experienced, mean and vain, but another and more powerful one, which has made
men of them, living tranquilly in the mud,
working and watching among the bullets,
with a hundred chances to one of being
killed, contrary to the common lot of their
kind. It is not for a cross, for rank; it is
not that they are threatened into submit-
ting to such terrible conditions of existence.
There must be another, a higher motive
power. This motive power is found in a
sentiment which rarely shows itself, which
is concealed with modesty, but which is deeply rooted in every Russian heart—patriotism. It is now only that the tales that circulated during the first period of the siege

of Sebastopol, when there were neither
fortifications, nor troops, nor material pos-
sibility of holding out there, and when,
moreover, no one admitted the thought of
surrender—it is now only that the anecdote
of Korniloff, that hero worthy of antique
Greece, who said to his troops, " Children,
we will die, but we will not surrender Sebastopol," and the reply of our brave soldiers, incapable of using set speeches, " We
will die, hurrah !"—it is now only that these
stories have ceased to be to you beautiful
historical legends, since they have become
truth, facts.　You will easily picture to yourself, in the place of those you have just seen,
the heroes of this period of trial, who never
lost courage, and who joyfully prepared to
die, not for the defence of the city, but for
the defence of the country.　Russia will long
preserve the sublime traces of the epoch of
Sebastopol, of which the Russian people
were the heroes !

Day closes; the sun, disappearing at the
horizon, shines through the gray clouds
which surround it, and lights up with purple rays the rippling sea with its green reflections, covered with ships and boats, the

white houses of the city, and the population stirring there. On the boulevard a regimental band is playing an old waltz, which sounds far over the water, and to which the cannonade of the bastions forms a strange and striking accompaniment.

SEBASTOPOL IN MAY, 1855

SEBASTOPOL IN MAY, 1855.

Six months had rolled by since the first bomb-shell thrown from the bastions of Sebastopol ploughed up the soil and cast it upon the enemy's works. Since that time millions of bombs, bullets, and balls had never ceased flying from bastions to trenches, from trenches to bastions, and the angel of death had constantly hovered over them.

The self-love of thousands of human beings had been sometimes wounded, sometimes satisfied, sometimes soothed in the embrace of death! What numbers of red coffins with coarse palls!—and the bastions still continued to roar. The French in their camp, moved by an involuntary feeling of anxiety and terror, examined in the soft evening light the yellow and burrowed earth of the bastions of Sebastopol, where the black silhouettes of our sailors came and went; they counted the embrasures bristling with fierce-looking cannon. On the telegraph tower an under-officer was watching through his field-glass the enemy's soldiers, their batteries, their tents, the movements of their troops on the Mamelon-Vert, and the smoke ascending from the trenches. A crowd composed of heterogeneous races, moved by quite different desires, converged from all parts of the world towards this fatal spot. Powder and blood had not succeeded in solving the question which diplomats could not settle.

I.

A regimental band was playing in the besieged city of Sebastopol; a crowd of soldiers and women in Sunday best was promenading in the avenues. The clear sun of spring had risen upon the English works, had passed over the fortifications, over the city, and over the Nicholas barracks, shedding everywhere its just and joyous light; now it was setting into the blue distance of the sea, which gently rippled, sparkling with silvery reflections.

An infantry officer of tall stature and with a slight stoop, busy putting on gloves of doubtful whiteness, though still presentable, came out of one of the small sailor-

houses built on the left side of Marine
Street. He directed his steps towards the
boulevard, fixing his eyes in a distracted
manner on the toe of his boots. The expression of his ill-favored face did not de-
note a high intellectual capacity, but traits
of good-fellowship, good sense, honesty, and
love of order were to be plainly recognized
there. He was not well-built, and seemed
to feel some confusion at the awkwardness
of his own motions. He had a well-worn
cap on his head, and on his shoulders a light
cloak of a curious purplish color, under
which could be seen his watch-chain, his
trousers with straps, and his clean and well-
polished boots. If his features had not
clearly indicated his pure Russian origin
he would have been taken for a German,
for an aide-de-camp, or for a regimental bag-
gage-master—he wore no spurs, to be sure—
or for one of those cavalry officers who have
been exchanged in order to take active service. In fact, he was one of the latter, and
while going up to the boulevard he was
thinking of a letter he had just received
from an ex-comrade, now a landholder in
the Government of F——; he was thinking

of his comrade's wife, pale, blue-eyed Natacha, his best friend; he was especially recalling the following passage :

"When they bring us the *Invalide*,*
Poupka (that was the name the retired
uhlan gave his wife) rushes into the ante-
chamber, seizes the paper, and throws her-
self upon the sofa in the arbor † in the parlor, where we have passed so many pleasant
winter evenings in your company while
your regiment was in garrison in our city.
You can't imagine the enthusiasm with
which she reads the story of your heroic
exploits! 'Mikhaïloff,' she often says in
speaking of you, 'is a pearl of a man, and I
shall throw myself on his neck when I see
him again! *He is fighting in the bastions, he
is!* He will get the cross of St. George,
and the newspapers will be full of him.' Indeed, I am beginning to be jealous of you.
It takes the papers a very long time to get
to us, and although a thousand bits of news
fly from mouth to mouth, we can't believe
all of them. For example: your good

---

* The Military Gazette.—TRANS.
† A sort of arbor covered with ivy was then used in
most fashionable parlors.—TRANS.

friends the *musical girls* related yesterday
how Napoleon, taken prisoner by our cossacks, had been brought to Petersburg—you
understand that I couldn't believe that!
Then one of the officials of the war office, a
fine fellow, and a great addition to society
now our little town is deserted, assured us
that our troops had occupied Eupatoria,
thus preventing the French from communica-
ting with Balaklava; that we lost two hundred men in this business, and they about
fifteen thousand. My wife was so much
delighted at this that she celebrated it all
night long, and she has a feeling that you
took part in the action and distinguished
yourself."

In spite of these words, in spite of the ex-
pressions which I have put in italics and
the general tone of the letter, Captain Mi-
khailoff took a sweet and sad satisfaction in
imagining himself with his pale, provincial
lady friend. He recalled their evening conversations on *sentiment* in the parlor arbor,
and how his brave comrade, the ex-uhlan,
became vexed and disputed over games of
cards with kopek stakes when they succeeded in starting a game in his study, and how

his wife joked him about it. He recalled
the friendship these good people had shown
for him ; and perhaps there was something
more than friendship on the side of the pale
friend ! All these pictures in their familiar
frames arose in his imagination with mar-
vellous softness. He saw them in a rosy
atmosphere, and, smiling at them, he han-
dled affectionately the letter in the bottom
of his pocket.

These memories brought the captain involuntarily back to his hopes, to his dreams.
" Imagine," he thought, as he went along the
narrow alley, " Natacha's joy and astonish-
ment when she reads in the *Invalide* that I
have been the first to get possession of a
cannon, and have received the Saint George!
I shall be promoted to be captain-major : I
was proposed for it a long time ago. It
will then be very easy for me to get to be
chief of an army battalion in the course of
a year, for many among us have been killed,
and many others will be during this campaign. Then, in the next battle, when I
have made myself well known, they will in-
trust a regiment to me, and I shall become
lieutenant-colonel, commander of the Order

of Saint Anne—then colonel—" He was
already imagining himself general, honoring
with his presence Natacha, his comrade's
widow—for his friend would, according to
the dream, have to die about this time—
when the sound of the band came distinctly
to his ears. A crowd of promenaders at-
tracted his gaze, and he came to himself on
the boulevard as before, second-captain of
infantry.

II.

He first approached the pavilion, by the
side of which several musicians were playing. Other soldiers of the same regiment
served as music-stands by holding before
them the open music-books, and a small
circle surrounded them, quartermasters, un-
der-officers, nurses, and children, engaged in
watching rather than in listening. Around
the pavilion marines, aides-de-camp, officers
in white gloves were standing, were sitting,
or promenading. Farther off in the broad
avenue could be seen a confused crowd of
officers of every branch of the service, wom-
en of every class, some with bonnets on, the
majority with kerchiefs on their heads; oth-

ers wore neither bonnets nor kerchiefs, but, astonishing to relate, there were no old women, all were young. Below in fragrant paths shaded by white acacias were seen isolated groups, seated and walking.

No one expressed any particular joy at the sight of Captain Mikhaïloff, with the exception, perhaps, of Objogoff and Souslikoff, captains in his regiment, who shook his hand warmly. But the first of the two had no gloves; he wore trousers of camel's-hair cloth, a shabby coat, and his red face was covered with perspiration; the second spoke with too loud a voice, and with shocking freedom of speech. It was not very flattering to walk with these men, especially in the presence of officers in white gloves. Among the latter was an aide-de-camp, with whom Mikhaïloff exchanged salutes, and a staff-officer whom he could have saluted as well, having seen him a couple of times at the quarters of a common friend.

There was positively no pleasure in promenading with these two comrades, whom he met five or six times a day, and shook hands with them each time. He did not come to the band concert for that.

He would have liked to go up to the
aide-de-camp with whom he exchanged salutes, and to chat with those gentlemen, not
in order that Captains Objogoff, Souslikoff,
Lieutenant Paschtezky, and others might
see him in conversation with them, but simply because they were agreeable, well-in-
formed people who could tell him something.

Why is Mikhaïloff afraid? and why can't
he make up his mind to go up to them?
It is because he distrustfully asks himself
what he will do if these gentlemen do not
return his salute, if they continue to chat together, pretending not to see him, and if
they go away, leaving him alone among the
aristocrats. The word *aristocrat,* taken in
the sense of a particular group, selected with
great care, belonging to every class of society, has lately gained a great popularity
among us in Russia—where it never ought
to have taken root. It has entered into all
the social strata where vanity has crept in
—and where does not this pitiable weakness
creep in? Everywhere; among the merchants, the officials, the quartermasters, the
officers; at Saratoff, at Mamadisch, at Vi-

nitzy — everywhere, in a word, where men are. Now, since there are many men in a besieged city like Sebastopol, there is also a great deal of vanity; that is to say, *aristocrats* are there in large numbers, although death, the great leveller, hovers constantly over the head of each man, be he aristocrat or not.

To Captain Objogoff, Second - captain Mikhaïloff is an *aristocrat;* to Second-captain Mikhaïloff, Aide-de-camp Kalouguine is an *aristocrat*, because he is aide-de-camp, and says thee and thou familiarly to other aides-de-camp; lastly, to Kalouguine, Count Nordoff is an *aristocrat*, because he is aide-de-camp of the Emperor.

Vanity, vanity, nothing but vanity! even in the presence of death, and among men ready to die for an exalted idea. Is not vanity the characteristic trait, the destructive ill of our age? Why has this weakness not been recognized hitherto, just as small-pox or cholera has been recognized? Why in our time are there only three kinds of men — those who accept vanity as an existing fact, necessary, and consequently just, and freely submit to it; those who consider it an evil element, but one impossible to destroy; and those who act under its influence with unconscious servility? Why have Homer and Shakespeare spoken of love, of glory, and of suffering, while the literature of our century is only the interminable history of snobbery and vanity?

Mikhaïloff, not able to make up his mind, twice passed in front of the little group of *aristocrats.* The third time, making a violent effort, he approached them. The group was composed of four officers—the aide-de-camp Kalouguine, whom Mikhaïloff was acquainted with, the aide-de-camp Prince Galtzine, an *aristocrat* to Kalouguine himself, Colonel Neferdoff, one of the *Hundred and Twenty-two* (a group of society men who had re-entered the service for this campaign were thus called), lastly, Captain of Cavalry Praskoukine, who was also among the Hundred and Twenty-two. Happily for Mikhaïloff, Kalouguine was in charming spirits; the general had just spoken very confidentially to him, and Prince Galtzine, fresh from Petersburg, was stopping in his quarters, so he did not find it compromising to offer his hand to a second-captain. Praskoukine did not decide to do as much, although he had often met Mikhaïloff in the bastion, had drunk his wine and his brandy more than once, and owed him twelve rubles and a half, lost at a game of preference. Being only slightly acquainted with Prince Galtzine, he had no wish to call his attention to his intimacy with a simple second-captain of infantry. He merely saluted slightly.

"Well, captain," said Kalouguine, "when are we going back to the little bastion? You remember our meeting on the Schwartz redoubt? It was warm there, hey?"

"Yes, it was warm there," replied Mikhaïloff, remembering that night when, following the trench in order to reach the bastion, he had met Kalouguine marching with a grand air, bravely clattering his sword. "I would not have to return there until to-morrow, but we have an officer sick." And he was going on to relate how, although it was not his turn on duty, he thought he ought to offer to replace Nepchissetzky, because the commander of the eighth company was ill, and only an ensign remained, but Kalouguine did not give him time to finish.

"I have a notion," said he, turning towards Prince Galtzine, "that something will come off in a day or two."

"But why couldn't something come off to-day?" timidly asked Mikhaïloff, looking first at Kalouguine and then at Galtzine.

No one replied. Galtzine made a slight grimace, and looking to one side over Mikhaïloff's cap, said, after a moment's silence,

"What a pretty girl!—yonder, with the red kerchief. Do you know her, captain?"

"It is a sailor's daughter. She lives close by me," he replied.

"Let's look at her closer."

And Prince Galtzine took Kalouguine by the arm on one side and the second-captain on the other, sure that by this action he would give the latter a lively satisfaction. He was not deceived. Mikhaïloff was superstitious, and to have anything to do with women before going under fire was in his eyes a great sin. But on that day he was posing for a libertine. Neither Kalouguine nor Galtzine was deceived by this, however. The girl with the red kerchief was very much astonished, having more than once noticed that the captain blushed as he was passing her window. Praskoukine marched

behind and nudged Galtzine, making all
sorts of remarks in French; but the path
being too narrow for them to march four
abreast, he was obliged to fall behind, and in
the second file to take Serviaguine's arm—
a naval officer known for his exceptional bravery, and very anxious to join the group of
aristocrats. This brave man gladly linked
his honest and muscular hand into Praskoukine's arm, whom he knew, nevertheless,
to be not quite honorable. Explaining to
Prince Galtzine his intimacy with the sailor,
Praskoukine whispered that he was a well-
known, brave man; but Prince Galtzine, who
had been, the evening before, in the fourth
bastion, and had seen a shell burst twenty
paces from him, considered himself equal
in courage to this gentleman; also being
convinced that most reputations were exaggerated, paid no attention to Serviaguine.

Mikhaïloff was so happy to promenade in
this brilliant company that he thought no
more of the dear letter received from F——,
nor of the dismal forebodings that assailed
him each time he went to the bastion. He
remained with them there until they had
visibly excluded him from their conversa-

tion, avoiding his eye, as if to make him understand that he could go on his way alone. At last they left him in the lurch. In spite of that, the second-captain was so satisfied that he was quite indifferent to the haughty expression with which the yunker* Baron Pesth straightened up and took off his hat before him. This young man had become very proud since he had passed his first night in the bomb-proof of the fifth bastion, an experience which, in his own eyes, transformed him into a hero.

III.

No sooner had Mikhaïloff crossed his own threshold than entirely different thoughts came into his mind. He again saw his little room, where beaten earth took the place of a wooden floor, his warped windows, in which the broken panes were replaced by paper, his old bed, over which was nailed to the wall a rug with the design of a figure of

---

* A cadet. The yunker ranks between sergeant and second-lieutenant, and belongs to the class of commissioned officers. Both the title and the function are borrowed from the German (*junker*). The present spelling is adopted to represent more nearly the Russian pronunciation.—TRANS.

an amazon, his pair of Toula pistols, hanging
on the head-board, and on one side a second
untidy bed with an Indian coverlet belonging to the yunker, who shared his quarters.
He saw his valet Nikita, who rose from the
ground where he was crouching, scratching
his head bristling with greasy hair. He saw
his old cloak, his second pair of boots, and
the bundle prepared for the night in the
bastion, wrapped in a cloth from which pro-
truded the end of a piece of cheese and the
neck of a bottle filled with brandy. Suddenly he remembered he had to lead his
company into the casemates that very night.

"I shall be killed, I'm sure," he said to
himself; "I feel it. Besides, I offered to go
myself, and one who does that is certain to
be killed. And what is the matter with this
sick man, this cursed Nepchissetzky? Who
knows? Perhaps he isn't sick at all. And,
thanks to him, a man will get killed—he'll
get killed, surely. However, if I am not
shot I will be put on the list for promotion.
I noticed the colonel's satisfaction when I
asked permission to take the place of Nepchissetzky if he was sick. If I don't get
the rank of major, I shall certainly get the

Vladimir Cross. This is the thirteenth time I go on duty in the bastion. Oh, oh, unlucky number! I shall be killed, I'm sure; I feel it. Nevertheless, some one must go. The company cannot go with an ensign; and if anything should happen, the honor of the regiment, the honor of the army would be assailed. It is my duty to go—yes, my sacred duty. No matter, I have a presentiment—"

The captain forgot that he had this presentiment, more or less strong, every time he went to the bastion, and he did not know that all who go into action have this feeling, though in very different degrees. His sense of duty which he had particularly developed calmed him, and he sat down at his table and wrote a farewell letter to his father. In the course of ten minutes the letter was finished. He arose with moist eyes, and began to dress, repeating to himself all the prayers which he knew by heart. His servant, a dull fellow, three-quarters drunk, helped him put on his new coat, the old one he was accustomed to wear in the bastion not being mended.

"Why hasn't that coat been mended?

You can't do anything but sleep, you beast!"

"Sleep!" growled Nikita, "when I am running about like a dog all day long. I tire myself to death, and after that am not allowed to sleep!"

"You are drunk again, I see."

"I didn't drink with your money; why do you find fault with me?"

"Silence, fool!" cried the captain, ready to strike him.

He was already nervous and troubled, and Nikita's rudeness made him lose patience. Nevertheless, he was very fond of the fellow, he even spoiled him, and had kept him with him a dozen years.

"Fool! fool!" repeated the servant. "Why do you abuse me, sir—and at this time? It isn't right to abuse me."

Mikhaïloff thought of the place he was going to, and was ashamed of himself.

"You would make a saint lose patience, Nikita," he said, with a softer voice. "Leave that letter addressed to my father lying on the table. Don't touch it," he added, blushing.

"All right," said Nikita, weakening under the influence of the wine he had taken, at his own expense, as he said, and blinking his eyes, ready to weep.

Then when the captain shouted, on leaving the house, " Good-by, Nikita !" he burst forth in a violent fit of sobbing, and seizing the hand of his master, kissed it, howling all the while, and saying, over and over again, "Good-by, master !"

An old sailor's wife at the door, good woman as she was, could not help taking part in this affecting scene. Rubbing her eyes with her dirty sleeve, she mumbled something about masters who, on their side, have to put up with so much, and went on to relate for the hundredth time to the drunken Nikita how she, poor creature, was left a widow, how her husband had been killed during the first bombardment and his house ruined, for the one she lived in now did not belong to her, etc., etc. After his master was gone, Nikita lighted his pipe, begged the landlord's daughter to fetch him some brandy, quickly wiped his tears, and ended up by quarrelling with the old woman about a little pail he said she had broken.

" Perhaps I shall only be wounded," the captain thought at nightfall, approaching the bastion at the head of his company. "But where—here or there?"

He placed his finger first on his stomach and then on his chest.

"If it were only here," he thought, pointing to the upper part of his thigh, "and if the ball passed round the bone! But if it is a fracture it's all over."

Mikhaïloff, by following the trenches, reached the casemates safe and sound. In perfect darkness, assisted by an officer of the sappers, he put his men to work; then he sat down in a hole in the shelter of the parapet. They were firing only at intervals; now and again, first on our side and then on *his*, a flash blazed forth, and the fuse of a shell traced a curve of fire on the dark, starlit sky. But the projectiles fell far off, behind or to the right of the quarters in which the captain hid at the bottom of a pit. He ate a piece of cheese, drank a few drops of brandy, lighted a cigarette, and having said his prayers, tried to sleep.

IV.

Prince Galtzine, Lieutenant-colonel Neferdorf, and Praskoukine — whom nobody had invited, and with whom no one chatted, but who followed them just the same—left the boulevard to go and drink tea at Kalouguine's quarters.

" Finish your story about Vaska Mendel," said Kalouguine.

Having thrown off his cloak, he was sitting beside the window in a stuffed easy-chair, and unbuttoned the collar of his well-starched, fine Dutch linen shirt.

" How did he get married again ?"

" It's worth any amount of money, I tell you ! There was a time when there was nothing else talked about at Petersburg," replied Prince Galtzine, laughingly.

He left the piano where he had been sitting, and drew near the window.

" It's worth any amount of money! I know all the details—"

And gayly and wittily he set about relating the story of an amorous intrigue, which we will pass over in silence because it offers us little interest. The striking thing about these gentlemen was, that one of them seated in the window, another at the piano, and a third on a chair with his legs doubled up, seemed to be quite different men from what

they were a moment before on the boulevard.   No more conceit, no more of this
ridiculous affectation towards the infantry
officers.   Here between themselves they
showed out what they were—good fellows,
gay, and in high spirits.   Their conversation continued upon their comrades and
their acquaintances in Petersburg.

" And Maslovsky?"

" Which one — the uhlan or the horse-
guardsman?"

" I know them both.   In my time the
horse-guardsman was only a boy just out
of school.   And the oldest, is he a captain?"

" Oh yes, for a long time."

" Is he always with his Bohemian girl?"

" No, he left her—"

And the talk went on in this tone.

Prince Galtzine sang in a charming manner a gypsy song, accompanying himself
on the piano.   Praskoukine, without being
asked, sang second, and so well too that, to
his great delight, they begged him to do it
again.

A servant brought in tea, cream, and rusks
on a silver tray.

"Give some to the prince," said Kalouguine.

" Isn't it strange to think," said Galtzine, drinking his glass of tea near the window, " that we are here in a besieged city, that we have a piano, tea with cream, and all this in lodgings which I would be glad to live in at Petersburg ?"

" If we didn't even have that," said the old lieutenant-colonel, always discontented, " existence would be intolerable. This continual expectation of something, or this seeing people killed every day without stopping, and this living in the mud without the least comfort—"

" But our infantry officers," interrupted Kalouguine, " those who live in the bastion with the soldiers, and share their soup with them in the bomb-proof, how do they get on ?"

" How do they get on ? They don't change their linen, to be sure, for ten days at a time, but they are astonishing fellows, true heroes !"

Just at this moment an infantry officer entered the room.

" I—I have received an order—to go to

general—to his Excellency, from General N——"he said, timidly saluting.

Kalouguine rose, and without returning the salute of the new-comer, without inviting him to be seated, begged him with cruel politeness and an official smile to wait a while; then he went on talking in French with Galtzine, without paying the slightest attention to the poor officer, who stood in the middle of the room, and did not know what to do with himself.

"I have been sent on an important matter," he said at last, after a moment of silence.

"If that is so, be kind enough to follow me." Kalouguine threw on his cloak and turned towards the door. An instant later he came back from the general's room.

"Well, gentlemen, I believe they are going to make it warm to-night."

"Ah! what—a sortie?" they all asked together.

"I don't know, you will see yourselves," he replied, with an enigmatic smile.

"My chief is in the bastion, I must go there," said Praskoukine, putting on his sword.

No one replied; he ought to know what he had to do. Praskoukine and Neferdorf went out to go to their posts.

" Good-by, gentlemen, *au revoir !* we will meet again to - night," cried Kalouguine through the window, while they set out at a rapid trot, bending over the pommels of their Cossack saddles. The sound of their horses' shoes quickly died away in the dark street.

" Come, tell me, will there really be some-thing going on to - night?" said Galtzine, leaning on the window-sill near Kalouguine, whence they were watching the shells rising over the bastions.

" I can tell you, you alone. You have been in the bastions, haven't you ?"

Although Galtzine had only been there once he replied by an affirmative gesture.

" Well, opposite our lunette there was a trench"—and Kalouguine, who was not a specialist, but who was satisfied of the value of his military opinions, began to explain, mixing himself up and making wrong use of the terms of fortification, the state of our works, the situation of the enemy, and the plan of the affair which had been prepared.

"There! there! They have begun to fire heavily on our quarters; is that coming from our side or from *his*—the one that has just burst there?" And the two officers, leaning on the window, watched the lines of fire which the shells traced crossing each other in the air, the white powder-smoke, the flashes which preceded each report and illuminated for a second the blue-black sky; they listened to the roar of the cannonade, which increased in violence.

"What a charming panorama!" said Kalouguine, attracting his guest's attention to the truly beautiful spectacle. "Do you know that sometimes one can't tell a star from a bomb-shell?"

"Yes, it is true; I just took that for a star, but it is coming down. Look! it bursts! And that large star there yonder —what do they call it? One would say it was a shell!"

"I am so accustomed to them that when I go back to Russia a starry sky will seem to me to be sparkling with bomb-shells. One gets so used to it."

"Ought I not to go and take part in this sortie?" said Prince Galtzine, after a pause.

" My dear fellow, what an idea! Don't think of it. I won't let you go; you will have time enough."

" Seriously — do you think I ought not to?"

At this moment, right in the direction these gentlemen were looking, could be heard above the roar of artillery the rattle of a terrible fusillade; a thousand little flames spurted and sparkled along the whole line.

" Look, it is in full swing," said Kalouguine. " I can't calmly listen to this fusillade; it stirs my soul! They are shouting ' Hurrah !' " he added, stretching his ear towards the bastion, from which arose the distant and prolonged clamor of thousands of voices.

" Who is shouting ' Hurrah'—*he* or we ?"

" I don't know; but they are surely fighting at the sword's point, for the fusillade has stopped."

An officer on horseback, followed by a Cossack, galloped up under their window, stopped, and dismounted.

" Where do you come from ?"

" From the bastion, to see the general."

"Come, what is the matter? Speak!"

"They have attacked — have taken the quarters. The French have pushed forward their reserves—ours have been attacked—and there were only two battalions of them," said the officer, out of breath.

It was the same one who had come in the evening, but this time he went towards the door with confidence.

"Then we retreated?" asked Galtzine.

"No," replied the officer, in a surly tone, "a battalion arrived in time. We repulsed them, but the chief of the regiment is killed, and many officers besides. They want reinforcements."

So saying, he went with Kalouguine into the general's room, whither we will not follow them.

Five minutes later Kalouguine set out for the bastion on a horse, which he rode in the Cossack fashion, a kind of riding which seems to give a particular pleasure to the aides-de-camp. He was the bearer of certain orders, and had to await the definite result of the affair. As to Prince Galtzine, he, agitated by the painful emotions which the signs of a battle in progress usually excite in the idle spectator, hastily went out into the street to wander aimlessly to and fro.

V.

Soldiers carried the wounded on stretchers, and supported others under the arms. It was very dark in the streets; here and there shone the lights in the hospital windows or in the quarters of a wakeful officer. The uninterrupted sound of the cannonade and the fusillade came from the bastions, and the same fires still lighted up the black sky. From time to time could be recognized the gallop of a staff-officer, the groan of a wounded man, the steps and the voices of the stretcher-bearers, the exclamations of doting women who stood on the thresholds of their houses and watched in the direction of the firing.

Among these last we find our acquaintance Nikita, the old sailor's widow with whom he had made up, and the little daughter of the latter, a child of ten years.

" Oh, my God ! holy Virgin and Mother !" murmured the old woman, with a sigh ; and she followed with her eyes the shells which

flew through space from one point to another like balls of fire. "What a misfortune!
what a misfortune! The first bombardment
was not so hard. Look! one cursed thing
has burst in the outskirts of the town right
over our house!"

"No, it is farther off; they are falling in
Aunt Arina's garden," said the child.

"Where is my master! where is he now!"
groaned Nikita, still drunk, and drawling his
words. "No tongue can tell how I love my
master! If, God forbid, they commit the
sin of killing him, I assure you, good aunt,
I won't be answerable for what I may do!
Really, he is such a good master that—
There is no word to express it, you see. I
wouldn't exchange him for those who are
playing cards inside, true. Pooh!" concluded Nikita, pointing to the captain's
room, in which the yunker Yvatchesky had
arranged with the ensigns a little festival
to celebrate the decoration he had just received.

"What a lot of shooting-stars there are!
what a lot of shooting-stars there are!"
cried the child, breaking the silence which
followed Nikita's speech. "There! there!

another one is falling! What is that for? Say, mother."

" They'll destroy our cabin!" sighed the old woman, without replying.

" To-day," resumed the sing-song voice of the little prattler—" to-day I saw in uncle's room, near the wardrobe, an enormous ball; it had come through the roof and had fallen right into the room. It is so large that they can't lift it."

" The women who had husbands and money are gone away," continued the old woman. " I have only a cabin, and they are destroying that! Look! look how they are firing, the wretches! Lord, my God!"

" And just as we were coming out of uncle's house," the child went on, " a bomb-shell came straight down; it burst, and threw the earth on all sides; one little piece almost struck us!"

VI.

Prince Galtzine met in constantly increasing numbers wounded men borne on stretchers, others dragging themselves along on foot or supporting each other, and talking noisily.

"When they fell upon us, brothers," said the bass voice of a tall soldier who carried two muskets on his shoulder—"when they fell upon us, shouting 'Allah! allah!'* they pushed one another on. We killed the first, and others climbed over them. There was nothing to be done; there were too many of them—too many of them!"

"You come from the bastion?" asked Galtzine, interrupting the orator.

"Yes, your Excellency."

"Well, what happened there? Tell me."

"This happened, your Excellency — *his strength* surrounded us; he climbed on the ramparts and had the best of it, your Excellency."

"How? the best of it? But you beat them back?"

"Ah yes, beat them back! But when all *his strength* came down upon us, *he* killed our men, and no help for it!"

The soldier was mistaken, for the trenches were ours; but, strange but well-authenticated fact, a soldier wounded in a battle al-

---

* The Russian soldiers accustomed to fight the Turks and to hear their battle-cries, always tell that the French have the same shout, "Allah!"—TRANS.

ways believes it a lost and a terribly bloody
one.

"I was told, nevertheless, that you beat
him back," continued Galtzine, good - naturedly; "perhaps it was after you came
away. Did you leave there long ago?"

"This very moment, your Excellency.
The trenches must belong to him; *he* had
the upperhand—"

"Why, aren't you ashamed of yourselves?
Abandon the trenches! It is frightful," said
Galtzine, irritated by the indifference of the
man.

"What could be done when *he* had the
strength."

"Ah, your Excellency," said a soldier borne
on a stretcher, "why not abandon them,
when he has killed us all? If we had the
strength we would never have abandoned
them! But what was to be done? I had
just stuck one of them when I was hit—
Oh, softly, brothers, softly! Oh, for mercy's sake!" groaned the wounded man.

"Hold on; far too many are coming
back," said Galtzine, again stopping the tall
soldier with the two muskets. "Why don't
you go back, hey? Halt!"

The soldier obeyed, and took off his cap with his left hand.

"Where are you going to?" sternly demanded the prince, "and who gave you permission, good-for—" But coming nearer, he saw that the soldier's right arm was covered with blood up to the elbow.

"I am wounded, your Excellency."

"Wounded! where?"

"Here, by a bullet," and the soldier showed his arm; "but I don't know what hit me a crack there." He held his head down, and showed on the back of his neck locks of hair glued together by coagulated blood.

"Whose gun is this?"

"It is a French carbine, your Excellency; I brought it away. I wouldn't have come away, but I had to lead that small soldier, who might fall down;" and he pointed to an infantryman who was walking some paces ahead of them leaning on his gun and dragging his left leg with difficulty.

Prince Galtzine was cruelly ashamed of his unjust suspicions, and conscious that he was blushing, turned around. Without questioning or looking after the wounded

any more, he directed his steps towards the
field-hospital. Making his way to the entrance with difficulty through soldiers, lit-
ters, stretcher-bearers who came in with the
wounded and went out with the dead, Galtzine entered as far as the first room, took
one look about him, recoiled involuntarily,
and precipitately fled into the street. What
he saw there was far too horrible!

VII.

The great, high, sombre hall, lighted only
by four or five candles, where the surgeons
moved about examining the wounded, was
literally crammed with people. Stretcher-
bearers continually brought new wounded
and placed them side by side in rows on
the ground. The crowd was so great that
the wretches pushed against one another
and bathed in their neighbors' blood. Pools
of stagnant gore stood in the empty places ;
from the feverish breath of several hundred
men, the perspiration of the bearers, rose
a heavy, thick, fetid atmosphere in which
candles burned dimly in different parts of
the hall. A confused murmur of groans,

sighs, death-rattles, was interrupted by piercing cries. Sisters of Charity, whose calm faces did not express woman's futile and tearful compassion, but an active and lively interest, glided here and there in the midst of bloody coats and shirts, sometimes striding over the wounded, carrying medicines, water, bandages, lint. Surgeons with their sleeves turned up, on their knees before the wounded, examined and probed the wounds by the flare of torches held by their assistants, in spite of the terrible cries and supplications of the patients. Seated at a little table beside the door a major wrote the number 532.

"Ivan Bogoïef, private in the third company of the regiment from C——, *fractura femuris complicata!*" shouted the surgeon, who was dressing a broken limb at the other end of the hall. "Turn him over."

"Oh, oh, good fathers!" gasped the soldier, begging them to leave him in peace.

"*Perforatio capites.* Simon Neferdof, lieutenant-colonel of the infantry regiment from N——. Have a little patience, colonel. There is no way of— I shall be obliged to leave you there," said a third, who was fumbling with a sort of hook in the head of the unfortunate officer.

" In Heaven's name, get done quickly !"

"*Perforatio pectoris.* Sebastian Sereda, private—what regiment? But it is no use, don't write it down. *Moritur.* Carry him off," added the surgeon, leaving the dying man, who with upturned eyes was already gasping.

Forty or fifty stretcher - bearers awaited their burdens at the door. The living were sent to the hospital, the dead to the chapel. They waited in silence, and sometimes a sigh escaped them as they contemplated this picture.

VIII.

Kalouguine met many wounded on his way to the bastion. Knowing by experience the bad influence of this spectacle on the spirit of a man who is going under fire, he not only did not stop them to ask questions, but he tried not to notice those he met. At the foot of the hill he ran across a staff-officer coming down from the bastion full speed.

" Zobkine ! Zobkine ! one moment !"

" What ?"

" Where do you come from ?"

" From the quarters."

" Well, what is going on there? Is it hot ?"

" Terribly !"

And the officer galloped off. The fusillade seemed to grow less; on the other hand, the cannonade began again with renewed vigor.

" Hum—a bad business !" thought Kalouguine. He had an indefinite but very disagreeable feeling; he had even a presentiment, that is to say, a very common thought —the thought of death.

Kalouguine possessed self-love and nerves of steel. He was, in a word, what is commonly called a brave man. He did not give way to this first impression; he raised his courage by recalling the story of one of Napoleon's aides-de-camp, who came to his chief with his head bloody, after having carried an order with all speed.

" Are you wounded ?" asked the emperor.

" I crave pardon, sire, I am dead !" replied the aide-de-camp, and falling from his horse, died on the spot.

This anecdote pleased him. Putting himself in imagination in the place of the aide-de-camp, he lashed his horse, put on a still more " Cossack " gait, and rising in his stirrups to cast a look upon the platoon that followed him on a trot, he reached the place where they had to dismount. There he found four soldiers sitting on some rocks, smoking their pipes.

" What are you doing there ?" he cried.

" We have been carrying a wounded man, your Excellency, and we are resting," said one of them, hiding his pipe behind his back and taking off his cap.

" That's it—you are resting ! Forward ! to your post !"

He put himself at their head and proceeded with them along the trench, meeting wounded men at every step. On the top of the plateau he turned to the left and found himself, a few steps farther on, completely isolated. A piece of a shell whistled near him and buried itself in the trenches ; a mortar-bomb rising in the air seemed to fly straight for his breast. Seized by a sudden terror, he rushed on several steps and threw himself down. When the bomb had burst some distance off he was very angry with himself and got up. He looked around to see if any one had noticed him lying down; no one was near.

Let fear once get possession of the soul, and it does not readily yield its place to another sentiment. He who had boasted of never bowing his head, went along the trenches at a rapid pace, and almost on his hands and feet.

"Ah! it is a bad sign," thought he, as his foot tripped. "I shall be killed, sure!"

He breathed with difficulty; he was bathed with sweat, and he was astonished that he made no effort to overcome his fright. Suddenly, at the sound of a step which approached, he quickly straightened up, raised his head, clinked his sabre with a swagger, and lessened his pace. He met an officer of sappers and a sailor. The former shouted, "Lie down!" pointing to the luminous point of a bomb-shell, which came nearer, redoubling its speed and its brightness.

The projectile struck in the side of the trench. At the cry of the officer, Kalouguine made a slight, involuntary bow, then continued on his way without a frown.

" There's a brave fellow!" said the sailor
who coolly watched the fall of the bomb.
His practised eye had calculated that the
pieces would not fall into the trench. " He
wouldn't lie down !"

In order to reach the bomb-proof occupied by the commander of the bastion, Kalouguine had only one more open space to
pass when he felt himself again overcome
by a stupid fear. His heart beat as if it
would burst, the blood rushed to his head,
and it was only by a violent effort of self-
control that he reached the shelter at a
run.

" Why are you so out of breath?" asked
the general, after he had delivered the order
he brought.

" I walked very quickly, Excellency."

" Can I offer you a glass of wine ?"

Kalouguine drank a bumper and lit a
cigarette. The engagement was finished,
but a violent cannonade continued on both
sides. The commander of the bastion and
several officers, among them Praskoukine,
were assembled in the bomb-proof; they
were talking over the details of the affair.
The interior, covered with figured paper

with a blue ground, was furnished with a
lounge, a bed, a table covered with papers,
and decorated with a clock hanging on
the wall and an image, before which burned
a small lamp. Seated in this comfortable
room, Kalouguine saw all the marks of a
quiet life; he measured with his eye the
great beams of the ceiling half a yard thick;
he heard the noise of the cannonade, deaf-
ened by the bomb-proofs, and he could not
understand how he could have yielded twice
to unpardonable attacks of weakness. Angry with himself, he would have liked to expose himself to danger again to put his courage to the proof.

A naval officer with a great mustache
and a cross of Saint George on his staff
overcoat came at this moment to beg the
general to give him some workmen to repair two sand-bag embrasures in the battery.

"I am very glad to see you, captain," said
Kalouguine to the new-comer; "the general
charged me to ask you if your cannon can
fire grape into the trenches."

"One single gun," replied the captain,
with a morose air.

" Let's go and look at them !"

The officer frowned and growled out,

" I have just passed the whole night there, and I have come in to rest a little; can't you go there alone? You will find my second in command, Lieutenant Kartz, who will show you everything."

The captain had commanded this same battery for full six months, and it was one of the most dangerous posts. He had not left the bastion, indeed, since the beginning of the siege, and even before the construction of the bomb-proof shelters. He had gained among the sailors a reputation for invincible courage. On this account his refusal was a lively surprise to Kalouguine.

" That's what reputations are !" thought the latter. " Then I will go alone, if you allow me," he added aloud, in a mocking tone, to which the officer paid no attention.

Kalouguine forgot that this man counted six whole months of life in the bastion, while he, altogether, at different times, had not passed more than fifty hours there. Vanity, desire to shine, to get a reward, to make a reputation, even the delight in danger, incited him still more, while the captain had become indifferent to all that.   He had also made a show, had performed courageous deeds, had uselessly risked his life, had hoped for and had received rewards, had established his reputation as a brave officer. But to-day these stimulants had lost their power over him; he looked at things differently.   Well understanding that he had little chance of escaping death after six months in the bastions, he did not thoughtlessly risk his life, and limited himself to fulfilling strictly his duty.   In fact, the young lieutenant appointed to his battery only eight days ago, and Kalouguine to whom this lieutenant showed it in detail, seemed ten times braver than the captain.   Rising in each other's estimation, these two hung out of the embrasures and climbed over the ramparts.

His inspection ended, and as he was returning to the bomb-proof, Kalouguine ran against the general, who was going to the observation tower, followed by his staff.

" Captain Praskoukine," ordered the general, " go down, I beg, into the quarters on the right.   You will find there the second battalion from M—— which is working

down there. Order it to stop work, to retire without noise, and to rejoin its regiment
in the reserve force at the bottom of the
hill. You understand? Lead it yourself
to the regiment."

"I'm off," replied Praskoukine, and he
departed on the run.

The cannonade diminished in violence.

IX.

"Are you the second battalion of the
regiment from M——?" asked Praskoukine
of a soldier who was carrying sand-bags.

"Yes."

"Where is the commander?"

Mikhaïloff, supposing that the captain of
the company was wanted, came out of his
pit, raised his hand to his cap, and approached Praskoukine, whom he took for a commanding officer.

"The general orders you — you must—
you must retire at once—without any noise
—to the rear; that is, to the reserve force,"
said Praskoukine, stealthily looking in the
direction of the enemy's fire.

Having recognized his comrade, and having gained an idea of the manœuvre, Mi-

khaïloff dropped his hand and gave the order to the soldiers. They took their muskets, put on their coats, and marched off.

He who has never felt it cannot appreciate the joy which a man experiences at leaving, after three hours of bombardment, a
place as dangerous as the quarters were.
During these three hours Mikhaïloff, who,
not without reason, was thinking of death
as an inevitable thing, had the time to get
accustomed to the notion that he would
surely be killed, and that he no longer belonged to the living world. In spite of that,
it was by a violent effort that he kept from
running when he came out of the quarters
at the head of his company, side by side with
Praskoukine.

"*Au revoir! bon voyage!*" shouted the
major who commanded the battalion left
in the quarters. Mikhaïloff had shared his
cheese with him, both of them seated in a
pit in shelter of the parapet.

" The same to you; good-luck! It seems
to me it is getting quieter."

But scarcely had he uttered these words
than the enemy, who had doubtless noticed
the movement, began to fire his best; our

side replied, and the cannonade began again with violence. The stars were shining, but with little light, for the night was dark. The shots and the shell explosions alone lighted for an instant the surrounding objects. The soldiers marched rapidly and in silence, some hurrying past the others: only the regular sound of their steps could be heard on the hardened earth, accompanied by the incessant roar of the cannonade, the click of bayonets striking one another, the sigh or the prayer of a soldier: " Lord ! Lord !"

Occasionally a wounded man groaned, and a stretcher was called for. In the company which Mikhaïloff commanded, the artillery fire had disabled twenty-six men since the day before.

A flash illuminated the distant darkness of the horizon; the sentinel on the bastion cried, " Can—non !" and a ball, whistling over the company, buried itself in the ground, which it ploughed up, sending the stones flying about.

" The devil take them ! How slowly they march !" thought Praskoukine, who, following Mikhaïloff, was looking behind him at every step. "I could run ahead, since I have delivered the order— Indeed, no! they would say I was a coward! Whatever happens I will march along with them."

"Why is he following me?" said Mikhaïloff, on his side. "I always noticed he brings bad luck. There comes another, straight towards us. seems to me."

A few hundred steps farther on they met Kalouguine on his way to the quarters, bravely rattling his sword. The general had sent him to ask how the work went on, but at the sight of Mikhaïloff he said to himself that, instead of exposing himself to this terrible fire, he could just as well find out by asking the officer who came from there. Mikhaïloff gave him, in fact, all the details. Kalouguine accompanied him to the end of the path, and re - entered the trench which led to the bomb-proof.

"What's the news?" asked the officer, who was supping alone in the earthwork.

"Nothing. I don't believe there will be any more fighting."

"How! no more fighting? On the contrary, the general has just gone up to the bastion. A new regiment has arrived. Be-

sides — listen ! — the fusillade is beginning
again. Don't go. What's the use of it?"
added the officer, as Kalouguine made a
movement.

"Nevertheless, I ought to go," said the
latter to himself. "However, haven't I been
exposed to danger long enough to-day?
The fusillade is terrible."

"It is true," he continued aloud, "I had
better wait here."

Twenty minutes later the general came
back, accompanied by his officers, among
whom was the yunker, Baron Pesth, but
Praskoukine was not with them. Our
troops had retaken and reoccupied the
quarters. After having heard the details
of the affair, Kalouguine went out of the
shelter with Pesth.

X.

"You have some blood on your overcoat;
were you fighting hand-to-hand?" asked
Kalouguine.

"Oh! it is frightful! Imagine—" And
Pesth began to relate how he had led his
company after the death of his chief, how
he had killed a Frenchman, and how, with-

out his assistance, the battle would have
been lost.   The foundation of the tale, that
is, the death of the chief and the Frenchman killed by Pesth, was true, but the
yunker, elaborating the details, enlarged on
them and boasted.

He boasted without premeditation.   During the whole affair he had lived in a fan-
tastic mist, so much so that everything that
had happened seemed to him to have taken
place vaguely, God knows where or how,
and to belong to some one besides himself.
Naturally enough he tried to invent incidents to his own advantage.   However, this
is the way the thing happened :

The battalion to which he had been detailed to take part in the sortie remained
two hours under the enemy's fire, then the
commander said a few words, the company
chiefs began to move about, the troops left
the shelter of the parapet and were drawn
up in columns a hundred paces farther on.
Pesth was ordered to place himself on the
flank of the second company.   Neither understanding the situation nor the movement, the yunker, with restrained breath
and a prey to a nervous tremor which

ran down his back, placed himself at the
post indicated, and gazed mechanically before him into the distant darkness, expecting something terrible. However, the sentiment of fear was not the dominating one
in his case, for the firing had ceased. What
appeared to him strange, uncomfortable, was
to find himself in the open field outside the
fortifications.

The commander of the battalion once
more pronounced certain words, which were
again repeated in a low voice by the officers,
and suddenly the black wall formed by the
first company sank down.   The order to lie
down had been given; the second company did the same, and Pesth in lying down
pricked his hand with some sharp thing.
The small silhouette of the captain of the
second company alone remained standing,
and he brandished a naked sword without
ceasing to talk and to walk back and forth
in front of the soldiers.

"Attention, children! Show yourselves
brave men! No firing! get at the wretches with the bayonet! When I shout ' hurrah!' follow me—closely and all together—
we will show them what we can do. We

won't cover ourselves with shame, will we, children? For the Czar, our father!"

"What's the name of the company chief?" asked Pesth from a yunker next to him. "He is a brave one!"

"Yes, he's always so under fire. He is called Lissinkoffsky."

Just at this moment a flame spurted out, followed by a deafening report; splinters and stones flew in the air. Fifty seconds later one of the stones fell from a great height and crushed the foot of a soldier. A shell had fallen in the middle of the company, a proof that the French had noticed the column.

"Ah! you are sending us shells now! Let us get at you and you will taste the Russian bayonet, curse you!"

The captain shouted so loud that the commander of the battalion ordered him to be silent.

The first company rose up, after that the second; the soldiers took up their muskets and the battalion advanced.

Pesth, seized by a foolish terror, could not remember whether they marched far; he went on like a drunken man. Suddenly thousands of fires flashed on all sides, with whizzings and crackings. He gave a yell and ran forward, because they all yelled and ran; then he tripped and fell over something. It was the company chief, wounded at the head of his troops, who took the yunker for a Frenchman and seized his leg. Pesth pulled his feet away and got up. Some one threw himself on him in the darkness, and he was almost knocked over again. A voice shouted to him, " Kill him, then! What are you waiting for ?"

A hand seized his musket, the point of his bayonet buried itself in something soft.

" Ah! Dieu!"

These words were spoken in French, with an accent of pain and fright. The yunker knew he had just killed a Frenchman. A cold sweat moistened his whole body; he began to tremble, and threw down his musket. But that lasted only a second; the thought that he was a hero came to his mind. Picking up his gun, he left the dead man, running and shouting " Hurrah!" with the rest. Twenty steps farther on he reached the trench where our troops and the commander of battalion were.

" I have killed one !" said he to the latter.

" You are a brave fellow, baron," was the reply.

XI.

" Did you know that Praskoukine is dead?" said Pesth to Kalouguine on the way back.

" It isn't possible !"

" Why not? I saw him myself."

" Good-by; I am in a hurry."

" A lucky day !" thought Kalouguine, as he was entering his quarters. " For the first time I am lucky. It has been a brilliant affair; I have come out of it safe and sound; there must be recommendations for decoration. A sword of honor will be the least they can give me. Faith, I have well deserved it !"

He made his report to the general, and went to his room. Prince Galtzine was reading a book at the table, and had been waiting for him a long time.

It was with an inexpressible joy that Kalouguine found himself at home, far from danger. Lying on his bed in his nightshirt, he related to Galtzine the incidents of

the fight. These incidents naturally arranged themselves so as to make it appear
how he, Kalouguine, was a brave and capable officer. He discreetly touched on this
because no one could be ignorant of it, and
no one, with the exception of the defunct
captain Praskoukine, had the right to doubt
it. The latter, although he felt very much
honored to walk arm-in-arm with the aide-
de-camp, had told one of his friends in his
very ear the evening before that Kalouguine
—a very good fellow, however—did not like
to walk on the bastions.

We left Praskoukine coming back with
Mikhaïloff. He reached a less exposed
place and began to breathe again, when he
perceived, on turning around, the sudden
light of a flash. The sentinel shouted,
" Mor—tar !" And one of the soldiers who
followed added, " It is coming straight into
the bastion !" Mikhaïloff looked. The luminous point of the bomb-shell seemed to
stop directly over his head, exactly the moment when it was impossible to tell what
direction it was going to take. That was
for the space of a second. Suddenly, redoubling its speed, the projectile came

nearer and nearer. The sparks of the fuse could be seen flying out, the dismal hissing was plainly audible. It was going to drop right in the midst of the battalion. " To earth !" shouted a voice. Mikhaïloff and Praskoukine obeyed. The latter, with shut eyes, heard the shell fall somewhere on the hard earth very near him. A second, which appeared to him an hour, passed, and the shell did not burst. Praskoukine was frightened; then he asked himself what cause he had for fear. Perhaps it had fallen farther away, and he wrongly imagined that he heard the fuse hissing near him. Opening his eyes, he was satisfied to see Mikhaïloff stretched motionless at his feet; but at the same time he perceived, a yard off, the lighted fuse of the shell spinning around like a top. A glacial terror, which stifled every thought, every sentiment, took possession of his soul. He hid his face in his hands.

Another second passed, during which a whole world of thoughts, of hopes, of sensations, and of souvenirs passed through his mind.

" Whom will it kill? Me or Mikhaïloff,

or indeed both of us together? If it is I, where will it hit me? If in the head, it will be all over; if on the foot, they will cut it off, then I shall insist that they give me chloroform, and I may get well. Perhaps Mikhaïloff alone will be killed, and later I will tell how we were close together, and how I was covered with his blood. No, no! it is nearer me—it will be I!"

Then he remembered the twelve rubles he owed Mikhaïloff, and another debt left at Petersburg, which ought to have been paid long ago. A Bohemian air that he sang the evening before came to his mind. He also saw in his imagination the lady he was in love with in her lilac trimmed bonnet; the man who had insulted him five years before, and whom he had never taken vengeance on. But in the midst of these and many other souvenirs the present feeling — the expectation of death — did not leave him. "Perhaps it isn't going to explode!" he thought, and was on the point of opening his eyes with desperate boldness. But at this instant a red fire struck his eyeballs through the closed lids, something hit him in the middle of the chest with a terri-

ble crash. He ran forward at random, en-
tangled his feet in his sword, stumbled, and
fell on his side.

"God be praised, I am only bruised."

This was his first thought, and he wanted
to feel of his breast, but his hands seemed as
if they were tied. A vice griped his head,
soldiers ran before his eyes, and he mechanically counted them:

"One, two, three soldiers, and, besides, an
officer who is losing his cloak!"

A new light flashed; he wondered what
had fired. Was it a mortar or a cannon?
Doubtless a cannon. Another shot, more
soldiers—five, six, seven. They passed in
front of him, and suddenly he became terribly afraid of being crushed by them. He
wanted to cry out, to say that he was bruised,
but his lips were dry, his tongue was glued
to the roof of his mouth. He had a burn-
ing thirst. He felt that his breast was damp,
and the sensation of this moisture made him
think of water. . . . He would have liked to
drink that which drenched him.

"I must have knocked the skin off in
falling," he said to himself, more and more
frightened at the idea of being crushed by

the soldiers who were running in crowds
before him. He tried again to cry out,
 " Take me !—"
But instead of that he uttered a groan so
terrible that he was frightened at it himself.
Then red sparks danced before his eyes ;
it seemed as if the soldiers were piling
stones on him. The sparks danced more
rapidly, the stones piled on him stifled him
more and more. He stretched himself out,
he ceased to see, to hear, to think, to feel.
He had been killed instantly by a piece of
shell striking him full in the breast.

XII.

Mikhaïloff also threw himself down on
seeing the shell. Like Praskoukine, he
thought of a crowd of things during the
two seconds which preceded the explosion.
He said his prayers mentally, repeating,
 " May Thy will be done ! Why, O Lord,
am I a soldier ? Why did I exchange into
the infantry to make this campaign ? Why
did I not remain in the uhlan regiment, in
the province of F——, near my friend Natacha ? and now see what is going to happen
to me."

He began to count—"One, two, three, four," saying to himself that if the shell exploded on an even number he would live, if at an odd number he would be killed.

"It is all over, I am killed!" he thought, at the sound of the explosion, without thinking any more of odd or even. Struck on the head, he felt a terrible pain.

"Lord, pardon my sins!" he murmured, clasping his hands.

He tried to rise, and fell unconscious, face downward. His first sensation when he came to himself was of blood running from his nose. The pain in his head was much lessened.

"My soul is departing. What will there be over *yonder?* My God, receive my soul in peace! It is nevertheless strange," he reasoned, "that I am dying, and I can distinctly hear the footsteps of the soldiers and the sound of shots!"

"A stretcher this way! The company chief is killed!" cried a voice which he recognized, that of the drummer Ignatieff.

Some one raised him up by the shoulders; he opened his eyes with an effort and saw the dark-blue sky over his head, myriads of stars, and two shells flying through space as if they were racing with each other. He saw Ignatieff, soldiers loaded down with stretchers and with muskets, the slope of the intrenchment, and suddenly he understood he was still in the world.

A stone had slightly wounded him on the head. His first impression was almost a regret. He felt so well, so quietly prepared to go over *yonder*, that the return to reality, the sight of the shells, of the trenches, and of blood, was painful to him. The second impression was an involuntary joy at feeling himself alive, and the third was the desire to leave the bastion as quickly as possible. The drummer bandaged his chief's head and led him towards the field-hospital, supporting him under his arm.

"Where am I going, and what for?" thought the captain, coming to himself a little. "My duty is to remain with my company—all the more," whispered a little voice within him, "since it will shortly be out of range of the enemy's fire."

"It's no use, my friend," he said to the drummer, taking away his arm. "I won't go to the field-hospital; I will stay with my company."

"You had better let yourself be properly taken care of, your Excellency. It don't seem to be anything at first, but it may grow worse. Indeed, your Excellency—"

Mikhaïloff stopped, undecided what to do. He would have followed Ignatieff's advice, perhaps, but he saw what a number of wounded men crowded the hospital, almost all of them seriously hurt.

"Perhaps the doctor will make fun of my scratch," he said to himself, and without listening to the drummer's arguments he went with a firm step to join his company.

"Where is officer Praskoukine, who was beside me a short time ago?" he asked of the sub-lieutenant whom he found at the head of the company.

"I don't know; I think he was killed," hesitatingly replied the latter.

"Killed or wounded? Why, don't you know? He was marching with us. Why didn't you bring him off?"

"It wasn't possible in that furnace."

"Oh! why did you abandon a living man, Mikhaïl Ivanitch?" said Mikhaïloff, with a vexed tone. "If he is dead, we must bring off his body."

"How can he be alive? Indeed I tell you I went up to him, and I saw— What would you have? We scarcely had time to bring off our own men. Ah! the devils, how they are firing shell now!"

Mikhaïloff sat down, and held his head in his hands. The walk had increased the violence of the pain.

"No," said he, "we must certainly go and get him. Perhaps he is alive. It is our duty, Mikhaïl Ivanitch."

Mikhaïl Ivanitch did not reply.

"He didn't think of bringing him off at the time, and now I must detail men for it. Why send them into this hell-fire, which will kill them, for nothing?" thought Mikhaïloff.

"Children, we must go back to get that officer who is wounded yonder in the ditch," he said, without raising his voice, and in a tone which had no authority, for he guessed how disagreeable the execution of this order would be to the men.

But since he addressed himself to no one in particular, not one of them came forward at this call.

"Who knows? he is dead, perhaps, and

it isn't worth while to risk our men uselessly. It is my fault; I ought to have thought
of it. I will go alone; it is my duty. Mikhaïl Ivanitch," he added, aloud, "lead on
the company, I will overtake you."

Gathering up the folds of his cloak with
one hand, he touched the image of St. Mi-
trophanes with the other. He wore this on
his breast as a sign of special devotion to
the blessed one.

The captain retraced his steps, assured
himself that Praskoukine was really dead,
and came back holding in his hand the
bandage which had become unwound from
his own head. The battalion was already at
the foot of the hill, and almost out of reach
of the balls, when Mikhaïloff rejoined it. A
few stray shells still came in their direction.

" I must go to-morrow and be registered
in the field - hospital," said the captain to
himself while the surgeon was dressing his
wound.

XIII.

Hundreds of mutilated, freshly bleeding
bodies, which two hours before were full of
hopes and of different desires, sublime or

humble, lay with stiffened limbs in the flow-
ery and dew-bathed valley which separated
the bastion from the intrenchment, or on
the smooth floor of the little mortuary chapel of Sebastopol. The dry lips of all of these
men murmured prayers, curses, or groans.
They crawled, they turned on their sides,
some were abandoned among the corpses
of the blossom-strewn valley, others lay on
stretchers, on cots, and on the damp floor
of the field-hospital. Notwithstanding all
this, the heavens shed their morning light
over Mount Saponné as on the preceding
days, the sparkling stars grew pale, a white
mist rose from the sombre and plaintively
swelling sea, the east grew purple with the
dawn, and long, flame-colored clouds stretched along the blue horizon. As on the days
before, the grand torch mounted slowly,
powerful and proud, promising joy, love, and
happiness to the awakened world.

XIV.

On the following evening the band of the
regiment of chasseurs again played on the
boulevard. Around the pavilion officers,
yunkers, soldiers, and young women prom-

enaded with a festal air in the paths of white
flowering acacias.

Kalouguine, Prince Galtzine, and another
colonel marched arm-in-arm along the street,
talking of the affair of the day before. The
chief subject of this conversation was, as it
always is, not of the affair itself, but of the
part the talkers had taken in it. The expression of their faces, the sound of their
voices, had something serious in it, and it
might have been supposed that the losses
profoundly affected them. But, to tell the
truth, since no one among them had lost
any one dear to him, they put on this offi-
cially mournful expression for propriety's
sake. Kalouguine and the colonel, although
they were very good fellows, would have
asked nothing better than to be present at
a similar engagement every day, in order to
receive each time a sword of honor or the
rank of major-general. When I hear a con-
queror who sends to their destruction millions of men in order to satisfy his personal
ambition called a monster, I always want
to laugh. Ask sub-lieutenants Petrouchef
Antonoff, and others, and you will see that
each is a little Napoleon, a monster ready

to engage in battle, to kill a hundred men, in order to obtain one more little star or an increase of pay.

" I ask pardon," said the colonel, " the affair began on the left flank. *I was there.*"

" Perhaps so," replied Kalouguine, "for I was almost all the time on the right flank. I went there twice, first to seek the general, then simply of my own accord to look on. It was there it was hot!"

" If Kalouguine says so it is a fact," continued the colonel, turning towards Galtzine. " Do you know that only to-day V—— told me you were a brave man? Our losses are truly frightful. In my own regiment four hundred men disabled! I don't understand how I came out alive."

At the other end of the boulevard they saw Mikhaïloff's bandaged head arise. He was coming to meet them.

" Are you wounded, captain?" asked Kalouguine.

" Slightly—by a stone," said Mikhaïloff.

" *Le pavillon est il déjà amené?*" said Prince Galtzine, looking over the head of the captain, and addressing himself to no one in particular.

"*Non pas encore,*" said Mikhaïloff, very anxious to show that he knew French.

"Does the armistice still go on?" asked Galtzine, addressing him politely in Russian, as if to say to the captain, "I know you speak French with difficulty, why not simply speak Russian?" Upon this the aides-de-camp went away from Mikhaïloff, who felt, as on the evening before, very lonesome. Not wishing to come in contact with some of them, and not making up his mind to approach others, he limited himself to saluting certain officers, and sat down near the Kazarsky monument to smoke a cigarette.

Baron Pesth also made his appearance on the boulevard. He related that he had taken part in the negotiations of the armistice, that he had chatted with the French officers, and that one of them had said to him,

"If daylight had come an hour later the ambuscades would have been retaken."

To which he had replied,

"Sir, I don't say they would not have been, so that I shall not contradict you," and his answer had filled him with pride.

In reality, although he had been present at the conclusion of the armistice, and had been very desirous of talking with the French, he had said nothing remarkable. The yunker simply promenaded for a long time in front of the lines, asking the nearest Frenchmen,

"What regiment do you belong to?"

They answered him, and that was all. As he advanced a little beyond the neutral zone, a French sentinel, who did not imagine that the Russian understood his language, flung a formidable curse at him.

"He is coming to examine our works, this damned—"

Indeed, after that the yunker returned home, composing along the road the French phrases he had just retailed to his acquaintances.

Captain Zobkine was also seen on the promenade, shouting with a loud voice; Captain Objogoff, with his torn uniform; the captain of artillery, who asked no favors of any one; the yunker, in love—in a word, all the personages of the day before, swayed by the same eternal moving forces. Praskoukine, Neferdoff, and several others were alone absent. Nobody thought of them. Nevertheless, their bodies were neither washed, nor dressed, nor buried in the earth.

XV.

White flags are flying on our fortifications and in the French intrenchments. In the blossom-covered valley mutilated bodies, clothed in blue or in gray, with bare feet, lie in heaps, and the men are carrying them off to place them in carts. The air is poisoned by the odor of the corpses. Crowds of people pour out of Sebastopol and out of the French camp to witness this spectacle. The different sides meet each other on this ground with eager and kindly curiosity.

Listen to the words exchanged between them. On this side, in a small group of French and Russians, a young officer is examining a cartridge - box. Although he speaks bad French, he can make himself understood.

" And why that—that bird?" he asks.

" Because it is the cartridge-box of a regiment of the guard, sir. It is ornamented with the imperial eagle."

" And you—you belong to the guard?"

" Pardon, sir, to the sixth regiment of the line."

" And this — where was this bought?"

The officer points to the little wooden mouth-piece which holds the Frenchman's cigarette.

"At Balaklava, sir. It is only palm-wood."

"Pretty," replies the officer, obliged to make use of the few words he knew, and which, *nolens volens*, intruded themselves into the conversation.

"You will oblige me if you will keep that as a souvenir of this meeting."

The Frenchman throws away his cigarette, blows in the mouth-piece, and politely presents it to the officer with a salute. The latter gives him his in exchange. All the French and Russian by-standers smile and seem delighted.

Here comes a shrewd-looking infantryman in a red shirt, his overcoat thrown over his shoulders. His face is full of good spirits and curiosity. Accompanied by two comrades, their hands behind their backs, he approaches and asks a Frenchman for a light. The latter blows into his pipe, shakes it, and offers a light to the Russian.

"*Tabac bonn!*" says the soldier in the red shirt, and the by-standers smile.

"Yes, good tobacco—Turkish tobacco!"

answers the Frenchman; "and with you Russian tobacco good?"

"*Rouss bonn!*" repeats the soldier in the red shirt, and this time the spectators burst out laughing.

"*Français pas bonn, bonn jour, mousiou!*" continues the soldier, making a show of all he knew in French, laughing, and tapping on the stomach of the man who was talking with him. The Frenchmen also laugh.

"They are not pretty, these Russian B——," said a Zouave.

"What are they laughing at?" asks another, with an Italian accent.

"*Le caftan bonn!*" the bold soldier begins again, examining the embroidered uniform of the Zouave.

"To your places, *sacré nom!*" shouts a French corporal at this instant.

The soldiers sulkily disperse.

Nevertheless, our young cavalry lieutenant is strutting in a group of the enemy's officers.

"I knew Count Sasonoff well," says one of the latter. "He is one of the true Russian counts, such as we like."

"I also knew a Sasonoff," replies the cav-

alry officer, " but he wasn't a count, as far
as I know. He is a small, dark man about
your age."

" That's it, sir — that's he. Oh, how I
would like to see the dear count! If you
see him, give him my regards. Captain
Latour," he adds, bowing.

" What a miserable business we are carrying on! It was hot last night, wasn't it?"
continues the cavalry officer, anxious to keep
up the conversation, and pointing to the
corpses.

" Oh, sir, it is frightful. But what fine
fellows your soldiers are! It is a pleasure
to fight with fine fellows like that."

" It must be confessed that your fellows
are up to snuff also," replies the Russian
horseman, with a salute, satisfied that he has
given him a good answer.

But enough on this subject. Let us
watch that ten - year - old boy, with an old
worn cap on his head which doubtless belonged to his father, and with naked legs
and large shoes on his feet, dressed in a
pair of cotton trousers, held up by a single
brace. He came out of the fortifications at
the beginning of the truce. He has been

walking about ever since on the low ground, examining with stupid curiosity the French soldiers and the dead bodies lying on the ground.   He is gathering the little blue field-flowers with which the valley is strewn. He retraces his steps with a great bouquet, holding his nose so as not to smell the fetid odor that comes on the wind. Stopping near a heap of corpses, he looks a long time at a headless, hideous, dead man. After an examination, he goes near and touches with his foot the arm stretched stiffly in the air. As he presses harder on it the arm moves and falls into place. The boy gives a cry, hides his face in the flowers, and enters the fortifications, running at full speed.

Yes, flags of truce float over the bastions and on the intrenchments; the brilliantly shining sun is setting into the blue sea, which ripples and sparkles under the golden rays. Thousands of people assemble, look at each other, chat, laugh. These people, who are Christians, who profess to obey the great law of love and devotion, are looking at their work without throwing themselves down in repentance at the knees of Him who gave them life, and with life the fear of

death, the love of the good and the beautiful.
They do not embrace each other like brothers, and shed tears of joy and happiness!
We must at least take consolation in the
thought that we did not begin the war, that
we are only defending our country, our na-
tive land. The white flags are lowered; the
engines of death and of suffering thunder
once more ; again a flood of innocent blood
is shed, and groans and curses can be heard.

I have said what I have wanted to say for
this time at least, but a painful doubt over-
whelms me. It would have been better, perhaps, to have kept silent, for possibly what
I have uttered is among those pernicious
truths obscurely hidden away in every one's
soul, and which, in order to remain harm-
less, must not be expressed; just as old wine
must not be disturbed lest the sediment rise
and make the liquid turbid. Where, then,
in my tale do we see the evil we must avoid,
and the good towards which we must strive
to go? Where is the traitor? Where is the
hero? All are good and all are bad. It is
not Kalouguine with his brilliant courage,
his gentlemanly bravado, and his vanity—
the chief motive power of all his actions ; it

is not Praskoukine, an inoffensive cipher, although he fell on the battle-field for his faith, his ruler, and his country; nor timid Mikhaïloff; nor Pesth, that child with no conviction and no moral sense, who can pass for traitors or for heroes.

No; the hero of my tale, the one I love with all the power of my soul, the one I have tried to reproduce in all his beauty, just as he has been, is, and always will be beautiful, is Truth.

SEBASTOPOL IN AUGUST, 1855.

I.

TOWARDS the end of the month of August there was slowly moving along the stony Sebastopol road between Douvanka* and Baktchisaraï an officer's carriage of peculiar form, unknown elsewhere, which held a middle place in construction between a basket - wagon, a Jewish britchka, and a Russian cart.

In this carriage a servant, dressed in linen, with a soft and shapeless officer's cap on his head, held the reins. Seated behind him, on parcels and bags covered with a soldier's overcoat, was an officer in a summer cloak, small in stature, as well as could be judged from the position he was in, who was less remarkable for the massive squareness of his shoulders than for the thickness of his body between his chest and his back. His neck from the nape to the shoulder was

---

* The last station before Sebastopol.—TRANS.

heavy and largely developed, and the mus-
cles were firmly extended. What is commonly spoken of as a waist did not exist,
nor the stomach either, although he was far
from being fat; and his face, upon which
was spread a layer of yellow and unhealthy
sunburn, was noticeable by its thinness. It
would have passed for an attractive one
if it had not been for a certain bloating
of the flesh and a skin furrowed by deep
wrinkles, which, interweaving, distorted the
features, took away all freshness, and gave
a brutal expression. His small, brown, ex-
traordinarily keen eyes had an almost impudent look. His very thick mustache, which
he was in the habit of biting, did not extend
much in breadth. His cheeks and his chin,
which he had not shaved for two days,
were covered with a black and thick beard.
Wounded on the head by a piece of shell
on the 10th of May, and still wearing a
bandage, he felt, nevertheless, entirely cured,
and left the hospital at Sympheropol to join
his regiment, posted somewhere there in the
direction where shots could be heard; but
he had not been able to find out whether it
was at Sebastopol itself or at Severnaïa or at

Inkerman. The cannonade was distinctly
heard, and seemed very near when the hills
did not cut off the sound which was brought
by the wind. Occasionally a tremendous explosion shook the air and made you tremble
in spite of yourself. Now and then less violent noises, like a drum-beat, followed each
other at short intervals, intermingled with
a deafening rumble; or perhaps all was con-
founded in a hubbub of prolonged rolls, like
peals of thunder at the height of a storm
when the rain begins to fall. Every one
said, and indeed it could be heard, that the
violence of the bombardment was terrible.
The officer urged his servant to hasten.
They met a line of carts driven by Russian
peasants, who had carried provisions to Sebastopol, and who were on their way back,
bringing sick and wounded soldiers in gray
overcoats, sailors in black pilot-coats, volun-
teers in red fez caps, and bearded militiamen. The officer's carriage was forced to
stop, and he, grimacing and squinting his
eyes in the impenetrable and motionless
cloud of dust raised by the carts, which flew
into the eyes and ears on all sides, examined
the faces as they passed by.

" There is a sick soldier of our company,"
said the servant, turning towards his master and pointing to a wounded man.

Seated sidewise on the front of his cart
a Russian peasant, wearing his whole beard,
a felt cap on his head, was tying a knot in
an enormous whip, which he held by the
handle under his elbow. He turned his
back to four or five soldiers shaken and
tossed about in the vehicle. One of them,
his arm tied up, his overcoat thrown on over
his shirt, seated erect and firm, although
somewhat pale and thin, occupied the middle place. Perceiving the officer, he instinctively raised his hand to his cap, but remembering his wound, he made believe he wanted to scratch his head. Another one was
lying down beside him on the bottom of
the cart. All that could be seen of him was
his two hands clinging to the wooden bars,
and his two raised knees swinging nerve-
lessly like two hempen dish-rags. A third,
with swollen face, his head wrapped with a
cloth on which was placed his soldier's cap,
seated sidewise, his legs hanging outside and
grazing the wheel, was dozing, his hands
resting on his knees.

" Doljikoff !" the traveller shouted at him.

" Present !" replied the latter, opening his eyes and taking off his cap. His bass voice was so full, so tremendous, that it seemed to come out of the chest of twenty soldiers together.

" When were you wounded ?"

" Health to your Excellency !"* he cried with his strong voice, his glassy and swollen eyes growing animated at the sight of his superior officer.

" Where is the regiment ?"

"At Sebastopol, your Excellency. They are thinking of going away from there Wednesday."

" Where to ?"

"They don't know — to Severnaïa, no doubt, your Excellency. At present," he continued, dragging his words, "*he* is firing straight through everything, especially with shells, even away into the bay. *He* is firing in a frightful manner !—" And he added words which could not be understood ; but from his face and from his position it could

---

* This is the literal translation of the common phrase used by the soldiers in reply to a greeting from their superior officers.—TRANS.

be guessed that, with a suffering man's sense
of injury, he was saying something of a not
very consoling nature.

Sub-lieutenant Koseltzoff, who had just
asked these questions, was neither an officer
of ordinary stamp nor among the number of
those who live and act in a certain way because others live and act thus. His nature
had been richly endowed with inferior qual-
ities. He sang and played the guitar in an
agreeable manner, he conversed well, and
wrote with facility, especially official corre-
spondence, of which he had got the trick
during his service as battalion aide-de-camp.
His energy was remarkable, but this energy only received its impulse from self-
love, and although grafted on this second-
rate capacity, it formed a salient and characteristic trait of his nature. That kind of
self-love which is most commonly developed
among men, especially among military men,
was so filtered through his existence that he
did not conceive a possible choice between
" first or nothing." Self-love was then the
motive force of his most intimate enthusi-
asms. Even alone in his own presence
he was fond of considering himself supe-

rior to those with whom he compared himself.

"Come! I am not going to be the one to listen to 'Moscow's'* chatter!" murmured the sub-lieutenant, whose thoughts had been troubled somewhat by meeting the train of wounded; and the soldier's words, the importance of which was increased and confirmed at each step by the sound of the cannonade, weighed heavily on his heart.

"They are curious fellows these 'Moscows'— Come, Nicolaïeff, forward! you are asleep, I think," he angrily shouted at his servant, throwing back the lappels of his coat.

Nicolaïeff shook the reins, made a little encouraging sound with his lips, and the wagon went off at a trot.

"We will stop only to feed them," said the officer, "and then on the road — forward!"

II.

Just as he entered the street of Douvanka, where everything was in ruins, Sub-lieu-

---

* In certain regiments the officers nicknamed the soldiers "Moscow," half in scorn, half in kindly sport.— TRANS.

tenant Koseltzoff was stopped by a wagon-train of cannon-balls and shells going towards Sebastopol, which was halted in the middle of the road.

Two infantrymen, seated in the dust on the stones of an overthrown wall, were eating bread and watermelon.

"Are you going far, fellow-countryman?" said one of them, chewing his mouthful. He was speaking to a soldier standing near them with a small knapsack on his shoulder.

"We are going to join our company; we have come from the country," replied the soldier, turning his eyes from the watermelon and arranging his knapsack. "For three weeks we have been guarding the company's hay, but now they have summoned everybody, and we don't know where our regiment is to-day. They tell us that since last week our fellows have been at Korabelnaïa. Do you know anything about it, gentlemen?"

"It is in the city, brother, in the city," replied an old soldier of the wagon-train, busy cutting with his pocket-knife the white meat of an unripe melon. "We just came from there. What a terrible business, brother!"

"What is that, gentlemen?"

" Don't you hear how he is firing now? No shelter anywhere! It is frightful how many of our men *he* has killed!" added the speaker, making a gesture, and straightening up his cap.

The soldier on his travels pensively shook his head, clacked his tongue, took his short pipe out of its box, stirred up the half-burned tobacco with his finger, lighted a bit of tinder from the pipe of a comrade who was smoking, and lifting his cap, said,

" There is no one but God, gentlemen. We say good-by to you;" and putting his knapsack in place, went his way.

"Ah! it is better worth while to wait," said the watermelon eater, with tone of conviction.

" It is all the same," murmured the soldier, settling the knapsack on his back, and worming his way between the wheels of the halted carts.

III.

At the station for horses Koseltzoff found a crowd of people, and the first figure he perceived was the postmaster in person, very young and very thin, quarrelling with two officers.

" You will not only wait twenty-four hours
but ten times twenty-four hours. Generals
wait too," he said, with the evident wish to
stir them up in a lively manner. "And I
am not going to hitch myself in, you understand !"

" If this is so, if there are no horses, they
can't be given to any one. Why, then, are
they given to a servant who is carrying baggage ?" shouted one of the two soldiers,
holding a glass of tea in his hand.

Although he carefully avoided using personal pronouns, it could easily be guessed
that he would have liked to say thee and
thou to his interlocutor.

" I want you to understand, Mr. Postmaster," hesitatingly said the other officer,
" that we are not travelling for our pleasure. If we have been summoned it is because we are necessary. You can be sure
I will tell the general, for it really seems
as if you have no respect for the rank of
officer."

" You spoil my work every time, and you
are in my way," rejoined his comrade, half
vexed. "Why do you talk to him about
respect ? You have to speak to him in

another manner. Horses!" he suddenly shouted, "horses, this instant!"

"I wouldn't ask better than to give them to you, but where can I get them? I understand very well, my friend," continued the postmaster, after a moment of silence, and warming up by degrees as he gesticulated, "but what do you want me to do? Let me just "— and the officers' faces at once had a hopeful expression—"keep soul and body together to the end of the month, and then I won't be seen any longer. I would rather go to the Malakoff than remain here, God knows! Do what you like —but I haven't a single wagon in good condition, and for three days the horses haven't seen a handful of hay."

At these words he disappeared. Koseltzoff and the two officers entered the house.

"So!" said the elder to the younger with a calm tone, which strongly contrasted with his recent wrath. "We are already three months on the road. Let's wait. It is no misfortune; there isn't any hurry."

Koseltzoff with difficulty found in the room of the post-house, all smoky, dirty, and filled with officers and trunks, an empty cor-

ner near the window. He sat down there,
and, rolling a cigarette, began to examine
faces and to listen to conversations. The
chief group was placed on the right of the
entrance door, around a shaky and greasy
table on which two copper tea-urns, stained
here and there with verdigris, were boiling;
lump - sugar was strewn about in several
paper wrappings. A young officer without
a mustache, in a new Circassian coat, was
pouring water into a teapot; four others of
about his own age were scattered in different corners of the room. One of them, his
head placed on a cloak which served him as
a pillow, was sleeping on a divan; another,
standing near a table, was cutting roast mut-
ton into small mouthfuls for a one - armed
comrade. Two officers, one in an aide-de-
camp's overcoat, the other in a fine cloth
infantry overcoat, and carrying a saddle-bag,
were sitting beside the stove; and it could
be readily divined by the way they looked
at the others, by the manner the one with
the saddle-bag was smoking, that they were
not officers of the line, and that they were
very glad of it. Their manner did not be-
tray scorn but a certain satisfaction with

themselves, founded partly on their relations
with the generals, and on a feeling of supe-
riority developed to such a point that they
tried to conceal it from others. There was
also in the place a doctor with fleshy lips,
and an artilleryman with a German physi-
ognomy, seated almost on the feet of the
sleeper, busily counting money. Four men-
servants, some dozing, some fumbling in the
trunks and the packets heaped up near the
door, completed the number of those present, among whom Koseltzoff found not a
face he knew. The young officers pleased
him. He guessed at once from their appearance that they had just come out of school,
and this called to his mind that his young
brother was also coming straight therefrom
to serve in one of the Sebastopol batteries.
On the other hand, the officer with the saddle-bag, whom he believed he had met somewhere, altogether displeased him. He found
him to have an expression of face so antipa-
thetic and so insolent that he was going to
sit down on the large base of the stove, with
the intention of putting him in his proper
place if he happened to say anything disagreeable. In his quality of brave and hon-

orable officer at the front he did not like the staff-officers, and for such he took these at the first glance.

IV.

" It is bad luck," said one of the young fellows, " to be so near the end and not be able to get there. There will perhaps be a battle to-day, even, and we will not be in it."

The sympathetic timidity of a young man who fears to say something out of place could be guessed from the slightly sharp sound of his voice, and from the youthful rosiness which spread in patches over his fresh face.

The one-armed officer looked at him with a smile.

" You will have time enough, believe me," he said.

The young officer respectfully turning his eyes upon the thin face of the latter suddenly lighted up by a smile, continued to pour the tea in silence. And truly the figure, the position of the wounded man, and, above all, the fluttering sleeve of his uniform, gave him that appearance of calm indifference which seemed to reply to everything said and done about him, "All this is very well, but I know it all, and I could do it if I wanted to."

"What shall we decide to do?" asked the young officer of his comrade with the Circassian coat. "Shall we pass the night here, or shall we push on with our single horse?

"Just think of it, captain," he continued, when his companion had declined his suggestion (he spoke to the one-armed man, picking up a knife he had dropped), "since they told us that horses could not be had at Sebastopol at any price, we bought one out of the common purse at Sympheropol."

"Did they skin you well?"

"I don't know anything about it, captain. We paid for the whole thing, horse and wagon, ninety rubles. Is it very dear?" he added, addressing all who looked at him, Koseltzoff included.

"It isn't too dear if the horse is young," said the latter.

"Isn't it? Nevertheless, we have been assured it was dear. He limps a little, it is true, but that will go off. They told us he was very strong."

"What institution are you from?" Koseltzoff asked him, wishing to get news of his brother.

"We belonged to the regiment of the nobility. There are six of us who are going of our own accord to Sebastopol," replied the loquacious little officer, "but we don't exactly know where our battery is. Some say at Sebastopol, but this gentleman says it is at Odessa."

"Wouldn't you have been able to find out at Sympheropol?" asked Koseltzoff.

"They didn't know anything there. Imagine it. They insulted one of our comrades who went to the government office for information! It was very disagreeable. Wouldn't you like to have this cigarette, already rolled?" he continued, offering it to the one-armed officer, who was looking for his cigar-case.

The young man's enthusiasm even entered into the little attentions he showered on him.

"You have also just come from Sebastopol?" he rejoined. "Heavens, how astonishing! At Petersburg we did nothing but think of you all, you heroes!" he added, turning to Koseltzoff with good-fellowship and respect.

" What if you are obliged to go back there ?" asked the latter.

" That's just what we are afraid of; for after having bought the horse and what we had to get — this coffee - pot, for example, and a few other trifles—we are left without a penny," he said, in a lower tone, casting a look at his companion on the sly, "so that we don't know how we are going to get out of it."

"You haven't received money on the road, then ?" Koseltzoff asked him.

" No," murmured the young man, "but they promised to give it to us here."

" Have you the certificate ?"

" I know the certificate is the chief thing. One of my uncles, a Senator at Moscow, could have given it to me, but I was assured I should receive it here without fail."

" Doubtless."

" I believe it also," replied the young officer, in a tone which proved that after having repeated the same question in thirty different places, and having received different replies everywhere, he no longer believed any one.

V.

"Who ordered beet soup?" shouted the house-keeper at this moment, a stout, slovenly dressed wench, about forty years old, who was bringing in a great earthen dish.

There was a general silence, and every eye was turned towards the woman. One of the officers even winked, exchanging with his comrade a look which plainly referred to the matron.

"But it was Koseltzoff who ordered it," rejoined the young officer; "we must wake him up. Halloo! come and eat," he added, approaching the sleeper and shaking him by the shoulder.

A youth of seventeen years, with black, lively, sparkling eyes and red cheeks, rose with a bound, and having involuntarily pushed against the doctor, said, "A thousand pardons!" rubbing his eyes and standing in the middle of the room.

Sub-lieutenant Koseltzoff immediately recognized his younger brother and went up to him.

"Do you know me?" he asked.

"Oh, oh, what an astonishing thing!" cried the younger, embracing him.

Two kisses were heard, but just as they were about to give each other a third, as the custom is, they hesitated a moment. It might have been said that each asked himself why he must kiss three times.

"How glad I am to see you!" said the elder, leading his brother outside. "Let's chat a bit."

"Come, come! I don't want any soup now. Eat it up, Féderson," said the youth to his comrade.

"But you were hungry—"

"No, I don't want it now."

Once outside on the piazza, after the first joyous outbursts of the youth, who went on to ask his brother questions without speaking to him of that which concerned himself, the latter, profiting by a moment of silence, asked him why he had not gone into the guard, as they had expected him to do.

"Because I wanted to go to Sebastopol. If everything comes out all right, I shall gain more than if I had remained in the guard. In that branch of the service you have to count ten years to the rank of colo-

nel, while here Todtleben has gone from
lieutenant-colonel to general in two years.
And if I am killed, well, then, what's to be
done ?"

" How you do argue," said the elder brother, with a smile.

"And then, that I have just told you is of
no importance.   The chief reason "—and he
stopped, hesitating, smiling in his turn, and
blushing as if he were going to say something very shameful—" the chief reason is
that my conscience bothered me.   I felt
scruples at living in Petersburg while men
are dying here for their country.   I counted
also on being with you," he added, still more
bashfully.

" You are a curious fellow," said the brother, without looking at him, hunting for his
cigar-case.   " I am sorry we can't stay together."

" Come, pray tell me the truth about the
bastions.   Are they horribly frightful ?"

" Yes, at first ; then one gets used to it.
You will see."

" Tell me also, please, do you think Sebastopol will be taken ?   It seems to me
that such a thing cannot happen."

" God only knows !"

" Oh, if you only knew how annoyed I am !
Imagine my misfortune. On the road I
have been robbed of different things, among
others my helmet, and I am in a fearful position. What will I do when I am presented to my chief ?"

Vladimir Koseltzoff, the younger, looked
very much like his brother Michael, at least
as much as a half-open columbine can
resemble one which has lost its flower.
He had similar blond hair, but thicker, and
curled around the temples ; while one long
lock strayed down the white and delicate
back of his neck ; a sign of happiness, as
the old women say. Rich young blood suddenly tinged his habitually dull complexion
at each impression of his soul ; a veil of
moisture often swept over his eyes, which
were like his brother's, but more open and
more limpid ; a fine blond down began to
show on his cheeks and on his upper lip,
which, purplish red in color, often extended
in a timid smile, exposing teeth of dazzling
whiteness. As he stood there in his unbuttoned coat, under which could be seen a
red shirt with Russian collar ; slender, broad-

shouldered, a cigarette between his fingers, leaning against the balustrade of the piazza, his face lighted up by unaffected joy, his eyes fixed on his brother, he was really the most charming and most sympathetic youth possible to see, and one looked away from him reluctantly.   Frankly happy to find his brother, whom he considered with pride and respect as a hero, he was, nevertheless, a little ashamed of him on account of his own more cultivated education, of his acquaintance with French, of his association with people in high places, and finding himself superior to him, he hoped to succeed in civilizing him. His impressions, his judgments, were formed at Petersburg under the influence of a woman who, having a weakness for pretty faces, made him pass his holidays in her house. Moscow had also contributed its part, for he had danced there at a great ball at the house of his uncle the Senator.

VI.

After having chatted so long as to prove, what often happens, that, while loving each other very much, they had few common interests, the brothers were silent for a moment or two.

"Come, get your traps and we'll go," said the elder.

The younger blushed and was confused.

"Straight away to Sebastopol?" he asked, at length.

"Of course. I don't believe you have many things with you; we will find a place for them."

"All right, we'll go," replied the younger, as he went into the house sighing.

Just as he was opening the door of the hall he stopped and held down his head.

"Go straight to Sebastopol," he said to himself, "be exposed to shells—it is terrible! However, isn't it all the same whether it is to-day or later? At least with my brother—"

To tell the truth, at the thought that the carriage would carry him as far as Sebastopol in a single trip, that no new incident would delay him longer on the road, he began to appreciate the danger he had come to meet, and the proximity of it profoundly moved him. Having succeeded in calming himself at last, he rejoined his comrades, and remained such a long time with them that

his brother, out of patience, opened the door
to call him, and saw him standing before the
officer, who was scolding him like a school-
boy.   At the sight of his brother his coun-
tenance fell.

"I'll come at once," he shouted, making
a gesture with his hand; "wait for me, I'm
coming!"

A moment later he went to find him.

"Just think," he said, with a deep sigh," I
can't go off with you."

"Stuff and nonsense!   Why not?"

"I am going to tell you the truth, Micha.
We haven't a penny; on the other hand,
we owe money to that captain.   It is horribly shameful!"

The elder brother scowled and kept silent.

"Do you owe much?" he asked at last,
without looking at him.

"No, not much; but it worries me awfully.
He paid three posts for me.   I used his sugar,
and then we played the game of preference,
and I owe him a trifle on that."

"That's bad, Volodia!   What would you
have done if you hadn't met me?" said the
elder, in a stern tone, never looking at him.

"But you know I count on receiving my

travelling expenses at Sebastopol, and then
I shall pay him. That can still be done;
and so I had rather go there with him to-
morrow."

At this moment the elder brother took a
purse out of his pocket, from which his trembling fingers drew two notes of ten rubles
each and one of three.

" Here's all I have," said he. " How much
do you want?" He exaggerated a little in
saying that it was all his fortune, for he still
had four gold-pieces sewn in the seams of
his uniform, but he had promised himself
not to touch them.

It was found, on adding up, that Koseltzoff
owed only eight rubles—the loss on the game
and the sugar together. The elder brother
gave them to him, making the remark that
one never ought to play when he had not
the wherewithal to pay. The younger said
nothing; for his brother's remark seemed
to throw a doubt on his honesty. Irritated,
ashamed of having done something which
could lead to suspicions or reflections on
his character on the part of his brother, of
whom he was fond, his sensitive nature was
so violently agitated by it that, feeling it im-

possible to stifle the sobs which choked him, he took the note without a word and carried it to his comrade.

VII.

Nikolaïeff, after refreshing himself at Douvanka with two glasses of brandy which he bought from a soldier who was selling it on the bridge, shook the reins, and the carriage jolted over the stony road which, with spots of shadow at rare intervals, led along Belbek to Sebastopol; while the brothers, seated side by side, their legs knocking together, kept an obstinate silence, each thinking about the other.

"Why did he offend me?" thought the younger. "Does he really take me for a thief? He seems to be still angry. Here we have quarrelled for good, and yet we two, how happy we could have been at Sebastopol! Two brothers, intimate friends, and both fighting the enemy — the elder lacking cultivation a little, but a brave soldier, and the younger as brave as he, for at the end of a week I shall have proved to all that I am no longer so young. I sha'n't blush any more; my face will be manly and

my mustache will have time to grow so far,"
he thought, pinching the down which was
visible at the corners of his mouth. "Perhaps we will get there to-day, even, and will
take part in a battle. My brother must be
very headstrong and very brave; he is one
of those who talk little and do better than
others. Is he continually pushing me on
purpose towards the side of the carriage?
He must see that it annoys me, and he
makes believe he does not notice it. We will
surely get there to-day," he continued to himself, keeping close to the side of the carriage,
fearing if he stirred that he would show his
brother he was not well seated. "We go
straight to the bastion—I with the artillery,
my brother with his company. Suddenly
the French throw themselves upon us. I
fire on the spot, I kill a crowd of them, but
they run just the same straight upon me.
Impossible to fire — I am lost! but my
brother dashes forward, sword in hand. I
seize my musket and we run together; the
soldiers follow us. The French throw themselves on my brother. I run up; I kill first
one, then another, and I save Micha. I am
wounded in the arm; I take my musket in

the other hand and run on.   My brother is
killed at my side by a bullet; I stop a moment, I look at him sadly, I rise and cry,
'Forward with me! let us avenge him!'   I
add, 'I loved my brother above everything;
I have lost him.   Let us avenge ourselves,
kill our enemies, or all die together!'   All
follow me, shouting.   But there is the whole
French army, Pélissier at their head.   We
kill all of them, but I am wounded once,
twice, and the third time mortally.   They
gather around me.   Gortschakoff comes and
asks what I wish for.   I reply that I wish
for nothing—I wish for only one thing, to
be placed beside my brother and to die with
him.   They carry me and lay me down beside his bloody corpse.   I raise myself up
and say, 'Yes, you could not appreciate
two men who sincerely loved their country.
They are killed — may God pardon you!'
and thereupon I die."

Who could tell to what point these dreams
were destined to be realized?

"Have you ever been in a hand-to-hand
fight?" he suddenly asked his brother, entirely forgetting that he did not want to
speak to him again.

" No, never. We have lost two thousand
men in our regiment, but always in the
works. I also was wounded there. War is
not carried on as you imagine, Volodia."

This familiar name softened the younger.
He wished to explain himself to his brother,
who did not imagine he had offended him.

" Are you angry with me, Micha?" he
asked, after a few moments.

" Why?"

" Because—nothing. I thought there had
been between us—"

" Not at all," rejoined the elder, turning
towards him and giving him a friendly tap
on the knee.

" I ask pardon, Micha, if I have offended
you," said the younger, turning aside to hide
the tears which filled his eyes.

VIII.

" Is this really Sebastopol?" asked Volodia, when they had reached the top of the
hill.

Before them appeared the bay with its
forest of masts, the sea, with the hostile
fleet in the distance, the white shore batteries, the barracks, the aqueducts, the docks,

the buildings of the city. Clouds of white
and pale lilac-colored smoke continually rose
over the yellow hills that surrounded the
city, and came out sharp against the clear
blue sky, lighted by the rosy rays, brilliantly reflected by the waves; while at the horizon the sun was setting into the sombre
sea.

It was without the least thrill of horror
that Volodia looked upon this terrible place
he had thought so much about. He experienced, on the contrary, an æsthetic joy, a
feeling of heroic satisfaction at thinking that
in half an hour he would be there himself,
and it was with profound attention that he
looked uninterruptedly, up to the very moment they arrived at Severnaïa, at this picture of such original charm. There was
the baggage of his brother's regiment, and
there also he had to find out where his own
regiment and his battery was.

The officer of the wagon-train lived near
to what they called the new little town, composed of board shanties built by sailors'
families. In a tent adjoining a shed of con-
siderable size, made of leafy oak branches
which had not yet time to wither, the broth-

ers found the officer sitting down in a shirt
of dirty yellow color before a rather slovenly
table, on which a cup of tea was cooling beside a plate and a decanter of brandy. A
few crumbs of bread and of caviare had fallen
here and there. He was carefully counting
a package of notes. But before bringing
him on the stage, we must necessarily examine closer the interior of his camp, his
duties, and his mode of life. The new hut
was large, solid, and conveniently built, provided with turf tables and seats, the same as
they build for the generals; and in order to
keep the leaves from falling, three rugs, in
bad taste, although new, but probably very
dear, were stretched on the walls and the
ceiling of the building. On the iron bed
placed under the principal rug, which repre-
sented the everlasting amazon, could be seen
a red coverlid of shaggy stuff, a soiled torn
pillow, and a cloak of cat-skin. On a table
were, helter-skelter, a mirror in a silver frame,
a brush of the same metal in a frightfully
dirty state, a candlestick, a broken horn comb
full of greasy hair, a bottle of liquor ornamented by an enormous red and gold label,
a gold watch with the portrait of Peter the

Great, gilt pen-holders, boxes holding per-
cussion-caps, a crust of bread, old cards
thrown about in disorder, and finally, under
the bed, bottles, some empty, others full. It
was the duty of this officer to look out for
the wagon-train and the forage for the
horses. One of his friends, occupied with
financial work, shared his dwelling, and was
asleep in the tent at this moment, while he
was making out the monthly accounts with
Government money. He had an agreeable
and martial appearance. He was distinguished by his great size, a large mustache,
and a fair state of corpulence. But there
were two unpleasant things in him which met
the eye at once. First, a constant perspiration on his face, joined with a puffiness which
almost hid his little gray eyes and gave him
the look of a leather bottle full of porter,
and, second, extreme slovenliness, which
reached from his thin gray hair to his great
naked feet, shod in ermine-trimmed slippers.

"What a lot of money!—heavens, what a
lot of money!" said Koseltzoff the first, who,
on entering, cast a hungry look on the notes.
"If you would lend me half, Vassili Mikhaïlovitch!"

The officer of the wagon-train looked sour at the sight of the visitors, and gathering up the money, saluted them without rising.

" Oh, if it were mine, but it is money belonging to the Crown, brother ! But whom have you there ?"

He looked at Volodia while he piled up the papers and put them in an open chest beside him.

" It is my brother just out of school. We come to ask where the regiment is."

" Sit down, gentlemen," he said, rising to go into the tent. " Can I offer you a little porter ?"

" I agree to porter, Vassili Mikhaïlovitch."

Volodia, on whom a profound impression was produced by the grand airs of the officer, as well as by his carelessness and by the respect his brother showed him, said to himself timidly, sitting on the edge of the lounge, " This officer, whom everybody respects, is doubtless a good fellow, hospitable, and probably very brave."

" Where is our regiment, then ?" asked the elder brother from the officer, who had disappeared in the tent.

" What do you say ?" shouted the latter.

The other repeated his question.

" I saw Seifer to-day," he replied; " he told me it was in the fifth bastion."

" Is it, sure ?"

" If I say so it is sure. However, devil take him! he lies cheaply enough! Say," he added, " will you have some porter?"

" I would gladly take a drink," replied Koseltzoff.

"And you, Ossip Ignatievitch," continued the same voice in the tent, addressing the sleeping commissary, "will you have a drink? You have slept enough; it is almost five o'clock."

" Enough of that old joke. You see well enough that I am not asleep," replied a shrill and lazy voice.

" Get up, then, for I am tired of it," and the officer rejoined his guests. " Give us some Sympheropol porter!" he shouted to his servant.

The latter, pushing against Volodia proudly, as it appeared to the young man, pulled out from under the bench a bottle of the porter called for.

The bottle had been empty some time, but the conversation was still going on, when

the flap of the tent was put aside to let pass
a small man in a blue dressing-gown with
cord and tassel, and a cap trimmed with
red braid and ornamented with a cockade.

With lowered eyes, and twisting his black
mustache, he only replied to the officer's salute by an imperceptible movement of the
shoulders.

" Give me a glass," he said, sitting down
near the table. " Surely you have just come
from Petersburg, young man ?" he said, addressing Volodia with an amiable air.

" Yes, and I am going to Sebastopol."

" Of your own accord ?"

" Yes."

" Why in the devil are you going, then ?
Gentlemen, really I don't understand that,"
continued the commissary. " It seems to
me, if I could, I would go back to Petersburg on foot. I have had my bellyful of
this cursed existence."

" But what are you grumbling at ?" asked
the elder Koseltzoff. " You are leading a
very enviable life here."

The commissary, surprised, cast a look at
him, turned around, and addressing Volodia, said, " This constant danger, these pri-

vations, for it is impossible to get anything—
all that is terrible. I really cannot understand you, gentlemen. If you only got some
advantage out of it! But is it agreeable, I
ask you, to become at your age good-for-
nothing for the rest of your days?"

"Some try to make money, some serve for
honor," replied Koseltzoff the elder, vexed.

"What is honor when there is nothing
to eat?" rejoined the commissary, with a dis-
dainful smile, turning towards the officer of
the wagon-train, who followed his example.
"Wind up the music-box," he said, pointing
to a box. "We'll hear ' Lucia ;' I like that."

"Is this Vassili Mikhaïlovitch a brave
man," Volodia asked his brother, when, twilight having fallen, they rolled again along
the Sebastopol road.

"Neither good nor bad, but a terribly mi-
serly fellow. As to the commissary, I can't
bear to see even his picture. I shall knock
him down some day."

IX.

When they arrived, at nightfall, at the
great bridge over the bay, Volodia was not
exactly in bad humor, but a terrible weight

lay on his heart. Everything he saw, everything he heard, harmonized so little with the
last impressions that had been left in his
mind by the great, light examination - hall
with polished floor, the voices of his comrades and the gayety of their sympathetic
bursts of laughter, his new uniform, the well-
beloved Czar, whom he was accustomed to
see during seven years, and who, taking
leave of them with tears in his eyes, had
called them "his children"—yes, everything
he saw little harmonized with his rich dreams
sparkling from a thousand facets.

"Here we are!" said his brother, getting
out of the carriage in front of the M——
battery. "If they let us cross the bridge
we will go straight to the Nicholas barracks. You will stop there until to-morrow
morning. As for me, I shall go back to my
regiment to find out where the battery is,
and to-morrow I will go and hunt you up."

"Why do that? rather let's go together,"
said Volodia. "I will go to the bastion
with you; won't that be the same thing?
One must get accustomed to it. If you go
there, why can't I go?"

"You would do better not to go."

"Let me go—please do. At least I will see what it is—"

"I advise you not to go there; but, nevertheless—"

The cloudless sky was sombre, the stars, and the flashes of the cannon, and the bombs flying in space, shone in the darkness. The *tête du pont* and the great white pile of the battery came out sharply in the dark night. Every instant reports, explosions, shook the air, together or separately, ever louder, ever more distinct. The mournful murmur of the waves played an accompaniment to this incessant roll. A fresh breeze filled with moisture blew from the sea. The brothers approached the bridge. A soldier awkwardly shouldered arms and shouted,

"Who comes there?"

"A soldier."

"You can't pass."

"Impossible—we must pass!"

"Ask the officer."

The officer was taking a nap, seated on an anchor. He arose and gave the order to let them pass.

"You can go in, but you can't come out. Attention! Where are you getting to all together?" he shouted to the wagons piled up with gabions, which were stopping at the entrance to the bridge.

On the first pontoon they met some soldiers talking in a loud voice.

" He has received his outfit; he has received it all."

"Ah! friends," said another voice, "when a fellow gets to Severnaïa he begins to revive. There is quite another air here, by heavens!"

" What nonsense are you talking there?" said the first. "The other day a cursed bomb-shell carried away the legs of two sailors. Oh! oh!"

The water in several places was dashing into the second pontoon, where the two brothers stopped to await their carriage. The wind, which had appeared light on land, blew here with violence and in gusts. The bridge swayed, and the waves, madly dashing against the beams, broke upon the anchors and the ropes and flooded the flooring. The sea roared with a hollow sound, forming a black, uniform, endless line, which separated it from the starry horizon, now lighted by a silvery glow. In the distance twinkled the lights of the hostile fleet. On the left rose the dark mass of a sailing ship, against the sides of which the water dashed violently; on the right, a steamer coming from Severnaïa, noisily and swiftly advanced. A bomb-shell burst, and lighted up for a second the heaps of gabions, revealing two men standing on the deck of the ship, a third in shirt-sleeves, sitting with swinging legs, busy repairing the deck, and showing the white foam and the dashing waves with green reflections made by the steamer in motion.

The same lights continued to furrow the sky over Sebastopol, and the fear-inspiring sounds came nearer. A wave driven from the sea broke into foam on the right side of the bridge and wet Volodia's feet. Two soldiers, noisily dragging their legs through the water, passed by. Suddenly something burst with a crash and lighted up before them the part of the bridge along which was passing a carriage, followed by a soldier on horseback. The pieces fell whistling into the water, which spouted up in jets.

"Ah, Mikhaïl Semenovitch!" said the

horseman, drawing up before Koseltzoff the
elder, "here you are—well again?"

"Yes, as you see. Where in God's name
are you going?"

"To Severnaïa for cartridges. They send
me in place of the aide-de-camp of the regiment. They are expecting an assault every
moment."

"And Martzeff, where's he?"

"He lost a leg yesterday in the city, in
his room. He was asleep. You know him,
perhaps."

"The regiment is in the fifth, isn't it?"

"Yes; it relieved the M——. Stop at
the field - hospital, you will find our fellows
there; they will show you the way."

"Have my quarters in the Morskaïa been
kept?"

"Ah, brother, the shells destroyed them
long since! You wouldn't recognize Sebastopol any longer. There isn't a soul there;
neither women, nor band, nor eating-house.
The last café closed yesterday. It is now
so dismal! Good-by!" and the officer went
away on the trot.

A terrible fear suddenly seized Volodia.
It seemed to him that a shell was going to

fall on him, and that a piece would surely strike him on the head. The moist darkness, the sinister sounds, the constant noise of the wrathful waves, all seemed to urge him to take not another step, and to tell him that no good awaited him there; that his foot would never touch the solid earth on the other side of the bay; that he would do well to turn back, to flee as quickly as possible this terrible place where death reigns. "Who knows? Perhaps it is too late. My lot is fixed." He said this to himself, trembling at the thought, and also on account of the water which was running into his boots. He sighed deeply, and kept away from his brother a little.

"My God! shall I really be killed—I? Oh, my God, have mercy on me!" he murmured, making the sign of the cross.

"Now we will push on, Volodia," said his companion, when their carriage had rejoined them. "Did you see the shell?"

Farther on they met more wagons carrying wounded men and gabions. One of them, filled with furniture, was driven by a woman. On the other side no one stopped their passage.

Instinctively hugging the wall of the Nicholas battery the two brothers silently went along it, with ears attentive to the noise of the shells which exploded over their heads and to the roar of the pieces thrown ·down from above; and at last they reached the part of the battery where the holy image was placed. There they learned that the Fifth Light Artillery Regiment, which Volodia was to join, was at Korabelnaïa. They consequently made up their minds in spite of the danger to go and sleep in the fifth bastion, and to go from there to their battery on the next day. Passing through the narrow passage, stepping over the soldiers who were sleeping along the wall, they at last reached the hospital.

X.

Entering the first room, filled with beds on which the wounded were lying, they were struck by the heavy and nauseating odor which is peculiar to hospitals. Two Sisters of Charity came to meet them. One of them, about fifty years old, had a stern face; she held in her hands a bundle of bandages and lint, and was giving orders to a very young assistant-surgeon who was following her. The other, a pretty girl of twenty, had a blond, pale, and delicate face. She appeared particularly gentle and timid under her little white cap; she followed her companion with her hands in her apron-pockets, and it could be seen that she was afraid of stopping behind. Koseltzoff asked them to show him Martzeff, who had lost a leg the day before.

"Of the P—— regiment?" asked the elder of the two sisters. "Are you a relative?"

"No, a comrade."

"Show them the way," she said in French to the younger sister, and left them, accompanied by the assistant-surgeon, to go to a wounded man.

"Come, come, what are you looking like that for?" said Koseltzoff to Volodia, who had stopped with raised eyebrows, and whose eyes, full of painful sympathy, could not leave the wounded, whom he watched without ceasing, at the same time following his brother, and repeating, in spite of himself, "Oh, my God! my God!"

"He has just come in, has he not?" the

young sister asked Koseltzoff, pointing to Volodia.

"Yes, he has just come."

She looked at him again and burst into tears, despairingly repeating, "My God! my God! when will it end?"

They entered the officers' room. Martzeff was there, lying on his back, his muscular arms bare to the elbow and held under his head. The expression on his yellow visage was that of a man who shuts his teeth tightly so as not to cry out with pain. His well leg, with a stocking on, stuck out from under the coverlid, and the toes worked convulsively.

"Well, how do you feel?" asked the young sister, raising the wounded man's hot head and arranging his pillow with her thin fingers, on one of which Volodia espied a gold ring. "Here are your comrades come to see you."

"I am suffering, you know," he replied, with an irritated air. "Don't touch me; it is well as it is," and the toes in the stocking moved with a nervous action. "How do you do? What's your name? Ah, pardon!" when Koseltzoff had told his name.

" Here everything is forgotten. Nevertheless we lived together," he added, without expressing the least joy, and looking at Volodia with a questioning air.

" It is my brother; he has just come from Petersburg."

"Ah! and I have done with it, I believe. Heavens, how I am suffering! If that would only stop quicker!"

He pulled his leg in with a convulsive movement. His toes worked with double restlessness. He covered his face with both hands.

" He must be left in quiet; he is very ill," the sister whispered to them. Her eyes were full of tears.

The brothers, who had decided to go to the fifth bastion, changed their minds on coming out of the hospital, and concluded, without telling each other the true reason, to separate, in order to not expose themselves to useless danger.

" Will you find your way, Volodia ?" asked the elder. " However, Nikolaïeff will lead you to Korabelnaïa. Now I am going alone, and to-morrow I will be with you."

That was all they said in this last interview.

XI.

The cannon roared with the same violence, but Ekaterinenskaïa Street, through which Volodia went, accompanied by Nikolaïeff, was empty and quiet. He could see in the darkness only the white walls standing in the midst of the great overthrown houses, and the stones of the sidewalk he was on. Sometimes he met soldiers and officers, and going along the left side, near the Admiralty, he noticed, by the bright light of a fire which burned behind a fence, a row of dark-leaved acacias, covered with dust, recently planted along the sidewalk and held up by green painted stakes. His steps and those of Nikolaïeff, who was loudly breathing, resounded alone in the silence. His thoughts were vague. The pretty Sister of Charity, Martzeff's leg, with his toes moving convulsively in his stocking, the darkness, the shells, the different pictures of death, passed confusedly in his memory. His young and impressionable soul was irritated and wounded by his isolation, by the complete indifference of every one to his lot, although he was exposed to danger.

"I shall suffer, I shall be killed, and no one will mourn me," he said to himself. Where, then, was the life of the hero full of the energetic ardor and of the sympathies he had so often dreamed of? The shells shrieked and burst nearer and nearer, and Nikolaïeff sighed oftener without speaking. In crossing the bridge which led to Korabelnaïa he saw something two steps off plunge whistling into the gulf, illuminating for a second with a purple light the violet-tinted waves, and then bound off, throwing a shower of water into the air.

"Curse it! the villain is still alive," murmured Nikolaïeff.

"Yes," answered Volodia, in spite of himself, and surprised at the sound of his own voice, so shrill and harsh.

They now met wounded men carried on stretchers, carts filled with gabions, a regiment, men on horseback. One of the latter, an officer followed by a Cossack, stopped at the sight of Volodia, examined his face, then, turning away, hit his horse with his whip and continued on his way. "Alone, alone! whether I am alive or not, it is the same to all!" said the youth to himself, ready to burst into tears. Having passed a great white wall, he entered a street bordered with little, quite ruined houses, continually lighted up by the flash of the shells. A drunken woman in rags, followed by a sailor, came out of a small door and stumbled against him. "I beg pardon, your Excellency," she murmured. The poor boy's heart was more and more oppressed, while the flashes continually lit up the black horizon and the shells whistled and burst about him. Suddenly Nikolaïeff sighed, and spoke with a voice which seemed to Volodia to express a restrained terror.

"It was well worth while to hurry from home to come here! We went on and went on, and what was the use of hurrying?"

"But, thank the Lord! my brother is cured," said Volodia, in order by talking to drive away the horrible feeling which had got possession of him.

"Finely cured, when he is in a bad way altogether! The well ones would find themselves much better off in the hospital in times like these. Do we, perchance, take any pleasure in being here? Now an arm is lost, now a leg, and then— And yet it is better here in the city than in the bastion, Lord God! On the way a man has to say all his prayers. Ah, scoundrel! it just hummed in my ears," he added, listening to the sound of a piece of shell which had passed close to him. "Now," continued Nikolaïeff, " I was told to lead your Excellency, and I know I must do what I am ordered to, but our carriage is in the care of a comrade, and the bundles are undone. I was told to come, and I have come. But if any one of the things we have brought is lost, it is I, Nikolaïeff, who answers for it."

A few steps farther on they came out on an open space.

" Here is your artillery, your Excellency," he suddenly said. "Ask the sentinel, he will show you."

Volodia went forward alone. No longer hearing behind him Nikolaïeff's sighs, he felt himself abandoned for good and all. The feeling of this desertion in the presence of danger, of death, as he believed, oppressed his heart with the glacial weight of a stone. Halting in the middle of the place, he looked all about him to see if he was observed, and taking his head in both hands, he murmured, with a voice broken by terror, " My God! am I really a despicable poltroon, a coward? I who have lately dreamed of dying for my country, for my Czar, and that with joy! Yes, I am an unfortunate and despicable being!" he cried, in profound despair, and quite undeceived about himself. Having finally overcome his emotion, he asked the sentinel to show him the house of the commander of the battery.

XII.

The commander of the battery lived in a little two-story house. It was entered through a court-yard. In one of the windows, in which a pane was missing and was replaced by a sheet of paper, shone the feeble light of a candle. The servant, seated in the door-way, was smoking his pipe. Having announced Volodia to his master, he showed him into his room. There, between two windows, beside a broken mirror, was seen a table loaded with official papers, several chairs, an iron bed with clean linen and a rug before it. Near the door stood the sergeant-major, a fine man, with a splendid pair of mustaches, his sword in its belt. On

his coat sparkled a cross and the medal of
the Hungary campaign. The staff-officer,
small in stature, with a swollen and bandaged cheek, walked up and down, dressed
in a frock - coat of fine cloth which bore
marks of long wear. He was decidedly corpulent, and appeared about forty years old.
A bald spot was clearly marked on the top
of his head; his thick mustache, hanging
straight down, hid his mouth; his brown
eyes had an agreeable expression; his
hands were fine, white, a little fat; his feet,
very much turned out, were put down with
a certain assurance and a certain affectation
which proved that bashfulness was not the
weak side of the commander.

"I have the honor to present myself. I
am attached to the Fifth Light Battery—
Koseltzoff, the second-ensign," said Volodia,
who, entering the room, recited in one breath
this lesson learned by heart.

The commander of the battery replied by
a somewhat dry salute, and without offering him his hand begged him to be seated.
Volodia then sat down timidly near the writ-
ing-table, and in his distraction getting hold
of a pair of scissors, began to play with them

mechanically. With hands behind his back and with bowed head, the commander of the battery continued his promenade in silence, casting his eyes from time to time on the fingers which continued to juggle with the scissors.

"Yes," he said, stopping at last in front of the sergeant-major, "from to-morrow on we must give another measure of oats to the caisson horses; they are thin. What do you think of it?"

"Why not? It can be done, your High Excellency; oats are now cheaper," replied the sergeant-major, his arms stuck to the side of his body and his fingers stirring—an habitual movement with which he usually accompanied his conversation.

"Then there is the forage-master, Frantzoné, who wrote me a line yesterday, your High Excellency. He said we must buy axle-trees without fail; they are cheap. What are your orders?"

"Well, they must be bought; there is money," answered the commander, continuing to walk. "Where are your traps?" he suddenly said, pausing before Volodia.

Poor Volodia, pursued by the thought

that he was a coward, saw in each look, in each word, the scorn he must inspire; and it seemed to him that his chief had already discovered his sad secret, and that he was jeering at him. Then he replied in confusion that his things were at Grafskaia, and that his brother would send them to him the following day.

"Where shall we put up the ensign?" the lieutenant-colonel asked the sergeant-major, without listening to the young man's answer.

"The ensign?" repeated the sergeant-major. A rapid glance thrown on Volodia, and which seemed to say, "What sort of an ensign is that?" finished the disconcerting of the latter. "Down there, your Excellency, with the second-captain. Since the captain is in the bastion his bed is empty!"

"Will that do for you while you are waiting?" asked the commander of the battery. "You must be tired, I think. To-morrow it can be more conveniently arranged for you."

Volodia arose and saluted.

"Will you have some tea?" added his superior officer. "The samovar can be heated."

Volodia, who had already reached the door, turned around, saluted again, and went out.

The lieutenant-colonel's servant conducted him down-stairs, and showed him into a bare and dirty room where different broken things were thrown aside as rubbish, and in which, in a corner, a man in a red shirt, whom Volodia took for a soldier, was sleeping on an iron bed without sheets or coverlid, wrapped in his overcoat.

"Peter Nikolaïevitch"—and the servant touched the sleeper's shoulder—"get up; the ensign is going to sleep here. It's Vlang, our yunker," he added, turning to Volodia.

"Oh, don't disturb yourself, I beg," cried the latter, seeing the yunker, a tall and robust young man, with a fine face, but one entirely devoid of intelligence, rise, throw his overcoat over his shoulders, and drowsily go away, murmuring, "That's nothing; I will go and sleep in the yard."

XIII.

Left alone with his thoughts, Volodia at first felt a return of the terror caused by the

trouble which agitated his soul. Counting
upon sleep to be able to cease thinking of
his surroundings and to forget himself, he
blew out his candle and lay down, covering
himself all up with his overcoat, even his
head, for he had kept his fear of darkness
since his childhood. But suddenly the idea
came to him that a shell might fall through
the roof and kill him. He listened. The
commander of the battery was walking up
and down over his head.

"It will begin by killing him first," he
said to himself, "then me. I shall not die
alone!" This reflection calmed him, and
he was going to sleep when this time the
thought that Sebastopol might be taken
that very night, that the French might
burst in his door, and that he had no weap-
on to defend himself, completely waked him
up again. He rose and walked the room.
The fear of the real danger had stifled the
mysterious terror of darkness. He hunted
and found to hand only a saddle and a
samovar. "I am a coward, a poltroon, a
wretch," he thought again, filled with disgust
and scorn of himself. He lay down and
tried to stop thinking; but then the im-

pressions of the day passed again through
his mind, and the continual sounds which
shook the panes of his single window recalled to him the danger he was in. Visions
followed. Now he saw the wounded covered with blood ; now bursting shells, pieces of
which flew into his room; now the pretty Sister of Charity who dressed his wounds weeping over his agony, or his mother, who, carrying him back to the provincial town, pray-
ing to God for him before a miraculous image, shed hot tears. Sleep eluded him ; but
suddenly the thought of an all - powerful
Deity who sees everything and who hears
every prayer flashed upon him distinct and
clear in the midst of his reveries. He fell
upon his knees, making the sign of the cross,
and clasping his hands as he had been
taught in his childhood. This simple gesture aroused in him a feeling of infinite, long-
forgotten calm.

"If I am to die, it is because I am useless! Then, may Thy will be done, O Lord!
and may it be done quickly. But if the
courage and firmness which I lack are necessary to me, spare me the shame and the
dishonor, which I cannot endure, and teach

me what I must do to accomplish Thy will."

His weak, childish, and terrified soul was fortified, was calmed at once, and entered new, broad, and luminous regions. He thought of a thousand things; he experienced a thousand sensations in the short duration of this feeling; then he quietly went to sleep, heedless of the dull roar of the bombardment and of the shaking windows.

Lord, Thou alone hast heard, Thou alone knowest the simple but ardent and despairing prayers of ignorance, the confused repentance asking for the cure of the body and the purification of the soul — the prayers which rise to Thee from these places where death resides; beginning with the general, who with terror feels a presentiment of approaching death, and a second after thinks only of wearing a cross of Saint George on his neck, and ending with the simple soldier prostrate on the bare earth of the Nicholas battery, supplicating Thee to grant him for his sufferings the recompense he unconsciously has a glimpse of.

XIV.

The elder Koseltzoff, having met a soldier of his regiment in the street, was accompanied by him to the fifth bastion.

" Keep close to the wall, Excellency," the
soldier said.

" What for ?"

" It is dangerous, Excellency. *He* is already passing over us," replied the soldier,
listening to the whistling of the ball, which
struck with a dry sound the other side of
the hard road. But Koseltzoff continued
on in the middle of the road without heeding this advice. There were the same streets,
the same but more frequent flashes, the same
sounds and the same groans, the same meeting of wounded men, the same batteries,
parapet, and trenches, just as he had seen
them in the spring. But now their aspect
was more dismal, more sombre and more
martial, so to speak. A greater number of
houses was riddled, and there were no more
lights in the windows — the hospital was
the only exception — no more women in
the street; and the character of the accustomed, careless life formerly imprinted on

everything was effaced, and was replaced by the element of anxious, weary expectation, and of redoubled and incessant effort.

He came at last to the farthermost intrenchment, and a soldier of the P—— regiment recognized his former company chief. There was the third battalion, as could be guessed in the darkness by the constrained murmur of voices and the clicks of the muskets placed against the wall, which the flash of the discharges lit up at frequent intervals.

" Where is the commander of the regiment ?" asked Koseltzoff.

" In the bomb-proof with the marines, your Excellency," replied the obliging soldier. " If you would like to go I will show you the way."

Passing from one trench to another, he led Koseltzoff to the ditch, where a sailor was smoking his pipe. Behind him was a door, through the cracks of which shone a light.

" Can we go in ?"

" I will announce you ;" and the sailor entered the bomb-proof, where two voices could be heard.

"If Prussia continues to keep neutral, then Austria—" said one of them.

"What is Austria good for when the slavs—" said the other.—"Ah yes! ask him to come in," added this same voice.

Koseltzoff, who had never before put his foot in these bomb-proof quarters, was struck by their elegance. A polished floor took the place of boards, a screen hid the entrance door. In a corner was a great icon representing the holy Virgin, with its gilt frame lighted by a small pink glass lamp. Two beds were placed along the wall, on one of which a naval officer was sleeping in his clothes, on the other, near a table on which two open bottles of wine were standing, sat the new regimental chief and an aide-de-camp. Koseltzoff, who was not bashful, and who felt himself in nowise guilty, either towards the State or towards the chief of the regiment, felt, nevertheless, at the sight of the latter—his comrade until very recently—a certain apprehension.

"It is strange," he thought, seeing him rise to listen to him. "He has commanded the regiment scarcely six weeks, and power is already visible in his bearing, in his look, in his clothes. Not a long while ago this same Batretcheff amused himself in our quarters, wore for whole weeks the same dark calico shirt, and ate his hash and his sour cream without inviting any one to share it, and now an expression full of hard pride can be read in his eyes, which say to me, 'Although I am your comrade, for I am a regimental chief of the new school, you may be sure I know perfectly well that you would give half your life to be in my place.'"

"You have been treating yourself to a rather long absence," said the colonel, coldly, looking at him.

"I have been ill, colonel, and my wound is not yet altogether healed."

"If that's so, what did you come back for?" Koseltzoff's corpulence inspired his chief with defiance. "Can you do your duty?"

"Certainly I can."

"All right. Ensign Zaïtzeff will conduct you to the ninth company, the one you have already commanded. You will receive the order of the day. Be so good as to send me the regimental aide-de-camp as you go out," and his chief, bowing slightly, gave him to understand by this that the interview was ended.

On his way out Koseltzoff muttered indistinct words and shrugged his shoulders several times. It might readily be believed that he felt ill at ease, or that he was irritated, not exactly against his regimental chief, but rather against himself and against all his surroundings.

XV.

Before going to find his officers he went to look up his company. The parapets built of gabions, the trenches, the cannon in front of which he passed, even the fragments and the shells themselves over which he stumbled, and which the flashes of the discharges lighted up without pause or relaxation, everything was familiar to him, and had been deeply engraven on his memory three months before, during the fortnight he had lived in the bastion. Notwithstanding the dismal side of these memories, a certain inherent charm of the past came out of them, and he recognized the places and things with an unaffected pleasure, as if the two weeks had been full of only agreeable impressions. His company was placed along the covered way which led to the sixth bastion.

Entering the shelter open on one side, he found so many soldiers there that he could scarcely find room to pass. At one end burned a wretched candle, which a reclining soldier was holding over a book that his comrade was spelling out. Around him, in the twilight of a thick and heavy atmosphere, several heads could be seen turned towards the reader, listening eagerly. Koseltzoff recognized the A B C of this sentence: " P-r-a-y-e-r a-f-t-e-r s-t-u-d-y. I give Thee thanks, my Cre-a-tor."

" Snuff the candle !" some one shouted. " What a good book !" said the reader, preparing to go on. But at the sound of Koseltzoff's voice calling the sergeant-major it was silent. The soldiers moved, coughed, and blew their noses, as always happens after an enforced silence. The sergeant-major arose from the middle of the group, buttoning his uniform, stepping over his comrades, and trampling on their feet, which for lack of room they did not know where to stow, approached the officer.

" How do you do, my boy? Is this our company?"

" Health to your Excellency! We congratulate you on your return," replied the sergeant - major, gayly and good - naturedly. " You are cured, Excellency? God be praised for that! for we missed you a good deal."

Koseltzoff, it was evident, was beloved by his company. Voices could immediately be heard spreading the news that the old company chief had come back, he who had been wounded—Mikhaïl Semenovitch Koseltzoff. Several soldiers, the drummer among others, came to greet him.

" How do you do, Obanetchouk?" said Koseltzoff. " Are you safe and sound? How do you do, children?" he then added, raising his voice.

The soldiers replied in chorus,

" Health to your Excellency!"

" How goes it, children?"

" Badly, your Excellency. The French have the upper hands. He fires from behind the intrenchments, but he doesn't show himself outside."

" Now, then, who knows? perhaps I shall

have the chance of seeing him come out of the intrenchments, children. It won't be the first time we have fought him together."

"We are ready to do our best, your Excellency," said several voices at the same time.

" He is very bold, then ?"

" Terribly bold," replied the drummer in a low tone, but so as to be heard, and speaking to another soldier, as if to justify his chief for having made use of the expression, and to persuade his comrade that there was nothing exaggerated nor untrue in it.

Koseltzoff left the soldiers in order to join the officers in the barracks.

XVI.

The great room of the barracks was filled with people—a crowd of naval, artillery, and infantry officers. Some were sleeping, others were talking, seated on a caisson or on the carriage of a siege-gun. The largest group of the three, seated on their cloaks spread on the ground, were drinking porter and playing cards.

"Ah! Koseltzoff's come back! Bravo! And your wound?" said divers voices from different sides.

Here also he was liked, and they were rejoiced at his return.

After having shaken hands with his acquaintances, Koseltzoff joined the gay group of card-players. One of them, thin, with a long nose, and a large mustache which encroached on his cheeks, cut the cards with his white, slender fingers on one of which was a great seal ring. He seemed disturbed, and dealt with an affected carelessness. On his right, lying half raised on his elbow, a gray-haired major staked and paid a half-ruble every time with exaggerated calmness. On his left, crouching on his heels, an officer with a red and shining face joked and smiled with an effort, and when his card was laid down, one of his hands moved in the empty pocket of his trousers He played a heavy game, but without any money—a fact which visibly irritated the dark officer with the handsome face. Another officer, pale, thin, and bald, with an enormous nose and a large mouth, walking about the room with a bundle of bank-notes in his hand, counted down the money on the bank and won every time.

Koseltzoff drank a small glass of brandy and sat down beside the players,

" Come, Mikhaïl Semenovitch, come ; put up your stake !" said the officer who was cutting the cards ; " I'll bet you have brought back a lot of money."

" Where could I have got it ? On the contrary, I spent my last penny in town !"

" Really ! You must have fleeced some one at Sympheropol, I'm sure !"

" What an idea !" replied Koseltzoff, not wanting his words to be believed, and un-buttoning his uniform, to be more comfort-able, he took a few old cards.

" I have nothing to risk, but, devil take me ! who can foresee luck ? A gnat can sometimes accomplish wonders ! Let's go on drinking to keep our courage up."

Shortly after he swallowed a second small glass of brandy, a little porter into the bar-gain, and lost his last three rubles, while a hundred and fifty were charged to the ac-count of the little officer with the sweat-moistened face.

" Have the kindness to send me the mon-ey," said the banker, interrupting the deal to look at him.

" Allow me to put off sending it until to-morrow," replied the one addressed, rising.

His hand was nervously moving in his empty pocket.

"Hum!" said the banker, spitefully throwing the last cards of the pack right and left. "We can't play in this way," he rejoined; "I will stop the game. It can't be done, Zakhar Ivanovitch. We are playing cash down, and not for credit."

"Do you distrust me? That would be strange indeed!"

"From whom have I to get eight rubles?" the major who had just won asked at this moment. "I have paid out more than twenty, and when I win I get nothing."

"How do you think I can pay you when there is no money on the table?"

"That's nothing to me!" cried the major, rising. "I am playing with you, and not with this gentleman!"

"As long as I tell you," said the perspiring officer—"as long as I tell you I will pay you to-morrow, how do you dare insult me?"

"I'll say what I like. This is no way of doing!" cried the major, excited.

"Come, be quiet, Fédor Fédorovitch!" shouted several players at once, turning around.

Let us drop the curtain on this scene. To-morrow, perhaps to-day, each of these men will go to meet death gayly, proudly, and will die calmly and firmly. The only consolation of a life the conditions of which freeze with horror the coldest imagination, of a life which has nothing human in it, to which all hope is interdicted, is forgetfulness, annihilation of the consciousness of the reality. In the soul of every man lies dormant the noble spark which at the proper time will make a hero of him; but this spark grows tired of shining always. Nevertheless, when the fatal moment comes, it will burst into a flame which will illumine grand deeds.

XVII.

The next day the bombardment continued with the same violence. About eleven o'clock in the forenoon Volodia Koseltzoff joined the officers of his battery. He became accustomed to these new faces, asked them questions, and, in his turn, shared his impressions with them. The modest but slightly pedantic conversation of the artillerymen pleased him and inspired his respect.

On the other hand, his own sympathetic appearance, his timid manner, and his simplicity predisposed these gentlemen in his favor. The oldest officer of the battery, a short, red-haired captain with a foretop, and with well-smoothed locks on his temples, brought up in the old traditions of artillery, amiable with ladies, and posing for a savant, asked him questions about his acquaintance with this science or that, about the new inventions, joked in an affectionate way about his youth and his handsome face, and treated him like a son, all of which charmed Volodia. Sub-lieutenant Dedenko, a young officer with an accent of Little Russia, with shaggy hair and a torn overcoat, pleased him also, in spite of his loud voice, his frequent quarrels, and his brusque movements, for under this rude exterior Volodia saw a brave and worthy man. Dedenko eagerly offered his services to Volodia, and tried to prove to him that the cannon at Sebastopol had not been placed according to rule. On the other hand, Lieutenant Tchernovitzky, with high-arched eyebrows, who wore a well-cared-for but worn and mended overcoat, and a gold chain on a satin waistcoat, did not inspire him with any sympathy, although superior to the others in politeness. He continually asked Volodia details about the emperor, the minister of war, related with factitious enthusiasm the heroic exploits accomplished at Sebastopol, expressed his regrets at the small number of true patriots, made a show of a great deal of knowledge, of wit, of exceedingly noble sentiments, but in spite of all that, and without being able to tell why, all these discourses sounded false in his ears, and he even noticed that the officers in general avoided speaking to Tchernovitzky. The yunker, Vlang, whom he had waked up the evening before, sat modestly in a corner, kept silent, laughed sometimes at a joke, always ready to recall what had been forgotten, presented to the officers in turn the small glass of brandy, and rolled cigarettes for all. Charmed by the simple and polite manners of Volodia, who did not treat him like a boy, and by his agreeable appearance, his great, fine eyes never left the face of the new-comer. Urged by a feeling of great admiration, he divined and forestalled all his wishes, a fact which the officers immediately noticed, and which furnished the subject of unsparing jokes.

A little before dinner second-captain Kraut, relieved from duty on the bastion, joined the little company. A blond, fine-looking fellow, of a lively turn of mind, proud possessor of a pair of red mustaches, and side-whiskers of the same color, he spoke the language to perfection, but too correctly and too elegantly for a pure-blooded Russian. Quite as irreproachable in duty as in his private life, perfection was his failing. A perfect comrade, to be counted on beyond proof in all affairs of interest, he lacked something as a man, just because everything in him was an accomplishment. In striking contrast with the ideal Germans of Germany, he was, after the example of the Russian Germans, in the highest degree practical.

"Here he is! here's our hero!" shouted the captain at the moment Kraut came in, gesticulating and clanking his spurs. "What'll you have, Frederic Christianovitch—tea or brandy?"

"I am having some tea made, but I won't refuse brandy while I am waiting, for my soul's consolation! Happy to make your acquaintance! Please get fond of us, and be well-disposed towards us," he said to Volodia, who had arisen to salute him. "Second-captain Kraut! The artificer told me you came last evening."

"Allow me to thank you for your bed, which I profited by last night."

"Did you at least sleep comfortably there? Because one of the legs is gone, and no one can repair it during the siege. You have to keep wedging it up."

"So then you got out of it safely?" Dedenko asked him.

"Yes, thank God! but Skvortzoff was hit. We had to repair one of the carriages; the side of it was smashed to pieces."

He suddenly arose and walked up and down. It could be seen that he felt the agreeable sensation of a man who has just come safe and sound out of great danger.

"Now, Dmitri Gavrilovitch," he said, tapping the captain's knee in a friendly manner, "how are you, brother? What has become of your presentation for advancement? Has it finally been settled?"

"No; nothing has come of it."

"And nothing will come of it," said Dedenko; "I've proved it to you already."

"Why will nothing come of it?"

"Because your statement is badly made."

"Ah, what a violent wrangler!" said Kraut,
gayly. "A truly obstinate Little Russian.
All right; you will see that they will make
you lieutenant to pay for your mortification."

"No, they won't do anything."

"Vlang," added Kraut, speaking to the
yunker, "fill my pipe and bring it to me,
please."

Kraut's presence had waked them all up.
Chatting with each one, he gave the details
of the bombardment, and asked questions
about what had taken place during his absence.

XVIII.

"Now, then, are you settled?" Kraut asked
of Volodia. "But, pardon me, what is your
name—both your names? It's our custom
in the artillery. Have you a saddle-horse?"

"No," answered Volodia, "and I am much
troubled about it. I have spoken to the
captain. I shall have neither horse nor
money until I get my forage-money and my

travelling expenses.   I would like to ask the
commander of the battery to lend me his
horse, but I am afraid he will refuse."

"You would like to ask this of Apollo
Serguéïtch?" said Kraut, looking at the captain, while he made a sound with his lips
which expressed doubt.

"Well," said the latter, "if he refuses,
there is no great harm done.   To tell the
truth, there is seldom need of a horse here.
I will undertake to ask him to-day even."

"You don't know him," said Dedenko.
"He would refuse anything else, but he
wouldn't refuse his horse to this gentleman.
Would you like to bet on it?"

"Oh, I know you are ripe for contradic-
tion, you—"

"I contradict when I know a thing!   He
isn't generous usually, but he will lend his
horse, because he has no interest in refus-
ing it."

"How no interest?   When oats cost eight
rubles here it is evidently in his interest.
He will have one horse the less to keep."

"Vladimir Semenovitch!" cried Vlang,
coming back with Kraut's pipe.   "Ask for
the spotted one; it is a charming horse."

"That's the one you fell into the ditch with, eh, Vlang?" observed the second-captain.

"But you are mistaken in saying that oats are eight rubles," maintained Dedenko, in the mean time, continuing the discussion. "According to the latest news they are ten-fifty. It is evident that there is no profit in—"

"You would like to leave him nothing, then? If you were in his place you would not lend your horse to go into town either. When I am commander of the battery my horses, brother, will have four full measures to eat every day! I sha'n't think of making an income, rest assured!"

"He who lives will see," replied the second-captain. "You will do the same when you have a battery, and he also," pointing to Volodia.

"Why do you suppose, Frederic Christianovitch, that this gentleman would also like to reserve for himself some small profit? If he has a certain amount of money, what will he do it for?" Tchernovitzky asked in his turn.

"No—I—excuse me, captain," said Volo-

dia, blushing up to his ears. "That would
be dishonest in my eyes."

"Oh! oh! what milk porridge!" Kraut
said to him.

"This is another question, captain, but
it seems to me that I couldn't take money for myself which doesn't belong to
me."

"And I will tell you something else," said
the second-captain, in a more serious tone.
"You must learn that, being battery commander, there is every advantage in manag-
ing affairs well. You must know that the
soldier's food doesn't concern him. It has
always been that way with us in the artillery. If you don't succeed in making both
ends meet, you will have nothing left. Let
us count up your expenses. You have first
the forage"—and the captain bent one finger; "next the medicine"—he bent a second one; "then the administration — that
makes three; then the draft-horses, which
certainly cost five hundred rubles — that
makes four; then the refitting of the soldiers' collars; then the charcoal, which is
used in great quantities, and at last the table of your officers; lastly, as chief of the

battery you must live comfortably, and you need a carriage, a cloak, etc."

"And the principal thing is this, Vladimir Semenovitch," said the captain, who had been silent up to this moment. " Look at a man like me, for example, who has served twenty years, receiving at first two, then three hundred rubles pay. Well, then, why shouldn't the Government reward him for his years of service by giving him a morsel of bread for his old days."

" It can't be discussed," rejoined the second-captain; " so don't be in a hurry to judge. Serve a little while and you will see."

Volodia, quite ashamed of the remark which he had thrown out without stopping to reflect, murmured a few words, and listened in silence how Dedenko set about defending the opposite thesis. The discussion was interrupted by the entrance of the colonel's orderly announcing that dinner was ready.

" You ought to tell Apollo Serguéitch to give us wine to-day," said Captain Tchernovitzky, buttoning his coat. " Devil take his avarice! He will be shot, and no one will get any."

" Tell him yourself."

" Oh no, you are my elder; the hierarchy before everything !"

XIX.

A table, covered with a stained table-cloth, was placed in the middle of the room in which Volodia had been received by the colonel the evening before. The latter gave him his hand, and asked him questions about Petersburg and about his journey.

" Now, gentlemen, please come up to the brandy. The ensigns don't drink," he added, with a smile.

The commander of the battery did not seem as stern to-day as the day before; he had rather the air of a kind and hospitable host than that of a comrade among his officers. In spite of that, all, from the old captain to Ensign Dedenko, evinced respect for him which betrayed itself in the timid politeness with which they spoke to him and came up in line to drink their little glass of brandy.

The dinner consisted of cabbage - soup, served in a great tureen in which swam lumps of meat with fat attached, laurel leaves, and a good deal of pepper, Polish *zrasi* with mustard, *koldouni* with slightly rancid butter; no napkins; the spoons were of pewter and of wood, the glasses were two in number. On the table was a single water decanter with broken neck. The conversation did not flag. They first spoke of the battle of Inkerman, in which the battery took a part. Each related his impressions, his opinions on the causes of the failure, keeping silent as soon as the battery commander spoke. Then they complained of the lack of cannon of a certain calibre; they talked of certain other improvements, which gave Volodia an opportunity of showing his knowledge. The curious part was that the talk did not even touch upon the frightful situation of Sebastopol, which seemed to mean that each one, on his part, thought too much about it to speak of it.

Volodia, very much astonished, and even vexed, that there was no question of the duties of his service, said to himself that he seemed to have come to Sebastopol only in order to give the details about the new cannon and to dine with the battery commander.

During the repast a shell burst very near

the house. The floor and the wall were shaken by it as by an earthquake, and powder-smoke spread over the window outside.

"You certainly didn't see that at Petersburg, but here we often have these surprises. Go, Vlang," added the commander, "and see where the shell burst."

Vlang went to look, and announced that it had burst in the yard. After that they did not speak of it again.

A little before the end of the dinner one of the military clerks came in to give to his chief three sealed envelopes. "This one is very urgent. A Cossack has just brought it from the commander of the artillery," he said. The officers watched the practised fingers of their superior with anxious impatience while he broke the seal of the envelope, which bore the words "in haste," and drew a paper from it.

"What can that be?" each one thought. "Can it be the order to leave Sebastopol for a rest, or the order to bring out the whole battery upon the bastion?"

"Once more!" cried the commander, angrily, throwing the sheet of paper on the table.

" What is it, Apollo Serguéïtch ?" asked
the oldest of the officers.

" They want an officer and men for a mortar battery. I have only four officers, and
my men are not up to the full number," he
growled, " and now they ask for some of
them. However, some one must go, gentlemen," he continued, after a moment ;
" they must be there at seven o'clock. Send
me the sergeant - major. Now, gentlemen,
who will go ? Decide it among yourselves."

" But here is this gentleman who hasn't
yet served," said Tchernovitzky, pointing to
Volodia.

" Yes ; I wouldn't ask for anything better," said Volodia, feeling a cold sweat moist-
en his neck and his backbone.

" No—why not ?" interrupted the captain.
" No one ought to refuse ; but it is useless
to ask him to go ; and since Apollo Serguéïtch leaves us free, we will draw lots, as
we did the other time."

All consented to this. Kraut carefully
cut several little paper squares, rolled them
up, and threw them into a cap. The captain cracked a few jokes and profited by
this occasion to ask the colonel for wine,

"to give us courage," he added.   Dedenko
had a depressed air, Volodia smiled, Tchernovitzky declared that he would be chosen
by the lot.   As to Kraut, he was perfectly
calm.

They offered Volodia the first chance.
He took one of the papers, the longest, but
immediately changed it for another, shorter
and smaller, and unrolling it, read the word
" Go."

" It is I," he said, with a sigh.

" All right.   May God protect you!   It
will be your baptism of fire," said the commander, looking with a pleasant smile at the
disturbed face of the ensign.   " But get
ready quickly, and in order that it may be
pleasanter, Vlang will go with you in the
place of the artificer.

XX.

Vlang, delighted with his mission, ran
away to dress, and came back at once to
assist Volodia to make up his bundles, ad-
vising him to take his bed, his fur cloak, an
old number of the " Annals of the Country,"
a coffee-pot with an alcohol lamp, and other
useless articles.   The captain, in his turn,

advised Volodia to read in the " Manual for
the use of Artillery Officers " the passage
relating to firing mortars, and to copy it at
once! Volodia set himself to work at it
immediately, happy and surprised to feel
that the dread of danger, especially the
fear of passing for a coward, was less strong
than on the evening before. His impressions of the day and his occupation had partly contributed to diminish the violence of
this; and then it is well known that an
acute sensation cannot last long without
weakening. In a word, his fear was being
cured. At seven in the evening, at the moment the sun was setting behind the Nicholas barracks, the sergeant-major came to
tell him that the men were ready, and were
waiting for him.

"I have given the list to Vlang, your Excellency; you can ask him for it," he said.

"Must I make a little speech to them?"
thought Volodia, on his way, accompanied
by the yunker, to join the twenty artillerymen who, swords by their sides, were waiting for him outside — " or must I simply
say to them, 'How do you do, children?' or,
indeed, say nothing at all? Why not say

' How do you do, children ?' I think I ought
to;" and with his full and sonorous voice he
cried boldly, " How do you do, children ?"
The soldiers replied cheerfully to his salu-
tation; his young and fresh voice sounded
agreeably in their ears.   He put himself at
their head, and although his heart was beat-
ing as if he had just run several furlongs,
his walk was light and his face was smiling.
When they got near the Malakoff mamelon,
he noticed, while climbing up it, that Vlang,
who did not leave his heels, and who had
seemed so courageous down below in their
quarters, stooped and ducked his head as
if the bullets and shells which were whistling without cessation were coming straight
towards him.   Several soldiers did the same,
and the majority of the faces expressed, if
not fear, at least disquiet.   This circum-
stance reassured him and revived his courage.

" Here I am, then, I also, on the Malakoff mamelon.   I imagined it a thousand
times more terrible, and I am walking, I am
advancing, without saluting the bullets !   I
am less afraid than the others, and I am
not a coward, then," he said to himself joy-

fully, with the enthusiasm of satisfied self-love.

This feeling was, however, shaken by the spectacle that presented itself to his eyes. When he reached in the twilight the Korniloff battery, four sailors, some holding by the legs, others by the arms, the bloody corpse of a man with bare feet and no coat, were in the act of throwing him over the parapet. (The second day of the bombardment they threw the dead into the ditch, because they had no time to carry them off.) Volodia, stupefied, saw the corpse strike the upper part of the rampart, and slide from there into the ditch. Fortunately for him, he met at this very moment the commander of the bastion, who gave him a guide to lead him to the battery and into the bomb-proof quarters of the men. We will not relate how often our hero was exposed to danger during that night. We will say nothing of how he was undeceived when he noticed that instead of finding them firing here according to the precise rules such as they practise at Petersburg on the plain of Volkovo, he saw himself in front of two broken mortars, one with its muzzle bruised by

a shell, the other still upright on the pieces
of a destroyed platform.   We will not tell
how it was impossible for him to get the
soldiers in order to repair it before daylight,
how he found no charge of the calibre indicated in the " Manual," nor describe his feelings at seeing two of his soldiers fall, hit
before his eyes, nor how he himself, even,
escaped death twenty times by a hair's-
breadth.   Happily for him, the captain of
the mortar, who had been given him for an
assistant, a tall sailor attached to these mortars since the beginning of the siege, assured
him that they could make use of them still,
and promised him while he was walking on
the bastion, lantern in hand, as calmly as
if he were in his kitchen-garden, to put them
in good condition before morning.

The bomb‑proof reduct into which his
guide conducted him was only a great, long
cavern dug in the rocky earth, two fathoms
deep, protected by oaken timbers eighteen
inches thick.   There he established himself
with his soldiers.

As soon as Vlang noticed the little low
door which led into it, he threw himself in
the first with such haste that he nearly fell

on the stone-paved floor, cowered down in
a corner, and did not care to come out of
it. The soldiers placed themselves on the
ground along the wall. Some of them lighted their pipes, and Volodia arranged his bed
in a corner, stretched himself on it, lighted
a candle in his turn, and smoked a cigarette.
Over their heads could be heard, deadened
by the bomb-proof, the uninterrupted roar of
the discharges. A single cannon close beside them shook their shelter every time it
thundered. In the interior everything was
quiet. The soldiers, still intimidated by the
presence of the new officer, only exchanged
a word with each other now and then to
ask for a light or a little room. A rat was
scratching somewhere among the stones,
and Vlang, who had not yet recovered from
his emotion, occasionally sighed deeply as he
looked about him. Volodia, on his bed in
this peaceful corner crammed with people,
lighted by a single candle, gave himself up
to the feeling of comfort which he had often
had as a child when, playing hide-and-seek,
he slipped into a wardrobe or under his
mother's skirt, holding his breath, stretching his ears, being very much afraid of the

dark, and feeling at the same time an unconscious impression of well-being.

In the same way here, without being altogether at his ease, he felt rather disposed
to be cheerful.

XXI.

At the end of ten minutes the soldiers
got bold and began to talk. Near the officer's bed, in the circle of light, were placed
the highest in rank—the two artificers, one
an old gray-haired man, his breast adorned
with a mass of medals and crosses, among
which the cross of Saint George was wanting, however, the other a young man, smoking cigarettes which he was rolling, and the
drummer, who placed himself, as is the custom, at the orders of the officer, in the back-
ground. In the shadow of the entrance,
behind the bombardier and the medalled
soldiers seated in front, the "humbles" kept
themselves. They were the first to break
silence. One of them, running in frightened from outside, served as a theme for
their conversation.

"Eh! say there, you didn't stay long in the
street. Young girls are not playing there,
hey?" said a voice.

"On the contrary, they are singing wonderful songs. You don't hear such ones in the village," replied the new-comer, with a laugh, and all out of breath.

"Vassina doesn't like the shells; no, he doesn't like them!" some one cried from the aristocratic side.

"When it is necessary it is another story," slowly replied Vassina, whom everybody listened to when he spoke. "The twenty-fourth, for example, they fired so that it was a blessing, and there is no harm in that. Why let us be killed for nothing? Do the chiefs thank us for that?"

These words provoked a general laugh.

"Nevertheless, there is Melnikoff, who is outside all the time," said some one.

"It is true. Make him come in," added the old artificer, "otherwise he will get killed for nothing."

"Who is this Melnikoff?" asked Volodia.

"He is, your Excellency, an animal who is afraid of nothing. He is walking about outside. Please examine him; he looks like a bear."

"He practises witchcraft," added Vassina, in his calm voice.

Melnikoff, a very corpulent soldier (a rare thing), with red hair, a tremendously bulging forehead, and light blue projecting eyes, came in just at this moment.

"Are you afraid of bomb-shells?" Volodia asked him.

"Why should I be afraid of them?" repeated Melnikoff, scratching his neck. "No bomb-shell will kill me, I know."

"Do you like to live here?"

"To be sure I do; it is very entertaining," and he burst out laughing.

"Then you must be sent out in a sortie. Would you like to? I will speak to the general," said Volodia, although he knew no general.

"Why not like to? I should like to very much!" and Melnikoff disappeared behind his comrades.

"Come, children, let's play 'beggar my neighbor!' Who has cards?" asked an impatient voice, and the game immediately began in the farthest corner. The calling of the tricks could be heard, the sound of taps on the nose and the bursts of laughter. Volodia in the mean time drank tea prepared by the drummer, offering some to the artificers, joking and chatting with them, desirous of making himself popular, and very well satisfied with the respect they showed him. The soldiers having noticed that the " barine " was a good fellow, became animated, and one of them announced that the siege was soon going to come to an end, for a sailor had told him for a certainty that Constantine, the Czar's brother, was coming to deliver them with the 'merican' * fleet; that there would soon be an armistice of two weeks to rest, and that seventy-five kopeks would have to be paid for every shot that was fired during the truce.

Vassina, whom Volodia had already noticed—the short soldier with fine great eyes and side-whiskers—related in his turn, in the midst of a general silence, which was next broken by bursts of laughter, the joy that had been felt at first on seeing him come back to his village on his furlough, and how his father had then sent him to work in the fields every day, while the lieutenant-forester sent to fetch his wife in a carriage. Volodia was amused by all these tales.   He

---

* American.

had no longer the least fear, and the strong odors which filled their reduct did not cause him any disgust. He felt, on the contrary, very gay, and in a very agreeable mood.

Several soldiers were snoring already. Vlang was also lying on the ground, and the old artificer, having spread his overcoat on the earth, crossed himself with devotion and mumbled the evening prayer, when Volodia took a fancy to go and see what was going on out of doors.

"Pull in your legs!" the soldiers immediately said to one another as they saw him get up, and each one drew his legs back to let him pass.

Vlang, who was supposed to be asleep, got up and seized Volodia by the lapel of his coat. "Come, don't go! what is the use?" he said, in a tearful and persuasive voice. "You don't know what it is. Bullets are raining out there. We are better off here."

But Volodia went out without heeding him, and sat down on the very threshold of their quarters by the side of Melnikoff.

The air was fresh and pure, especially after that he had just been breathing, and the

night was clear and calm. Through the
roar of the cannonade could be heard the
creak of the wheels of the carts bringing
gabions, and the voices of those working in
the magazine. Over their heads sparkled
the starry sky, striped by the luminous fur-
rows of the projectiles. On the left was
a small opening, two feet and a half high,
leading to a bomb-proof shelter, where could
be perceived the feet and the backs of the
sailors who lived there, and who were plainly heard talking. Opposite rose the mound
which covered the magazine, in front of
which figures, bent double, passed and re-
passed. On the very top of the eminence,
exposed to bullets and shells which did not
stop whistling at that spot, was a tall black
figure, with his hands in his pockets, trampling on the fresh earth which was brought
in bags. From time to time a shell fell and
burst two paces from him. The soldiers
who were carrying sacks bent down and
separated, while the black silhouette continued quietly to level the earth with his feet
without changing his position.

" Who is it?" Volodia asked Melnikoff.

" I don't know; I am going to see."

" Don't go ; it is no use."

But Melnikoff rose without listening to him, went up to the black man, and remained immovable a long time beside him with the same indifference to danger.

" It is the guardian of the magazine, your Excellency," he said, on his return. " A shell made a hole in it, and they are covering it up with earth."

When the shells seemed to fly straight upon the bomb-proof quarters Volodia squeezed himself into the corner, and then came out raising his eyes to the sky to see if others were coming. Although Vlang, still lying down, had more than once begged him to come in, Volodia passed three hours seated on the threshold, finding a certain pleasure in thus exposing himself, as well as in watching the flight of the projectiles. Towards the end of the evening he knew perfectly well the number of the cannon and the direction they fired, and where their shots struck.

XXII.

The next day—the 27th of August—after ten hours of sleep, Volodia came out of the bomb-proof fresh and well. Vlang followed him, but at the first hissing of a cannon-ball he bounded back and threw himself through the narrow opening, knocking his head as he went, to the general laugh of the soldiers, all of whom, with the exception of Vlang, of the old artificer, and two or three others who rarely showed themselves in the trenches, had slipped outside to breathe the fresh morning air. In spite of the violence of the bombardment, they could not be prevented from remaining there, some near the entrance, others sheltered by the parapet. As to Melnikoff, he had been going and coming between the batteries since daybreak, looking in the air with indifference.

On the very threshold of the quarters were seated three soldiers, two old and one young one. The latter, a curly-headed Jewish infantryman attached to the battery, picked up a bullet which rolled at his feet, and flattening it against a stone with a piece of a shell, he cut out of it a cross on the model of that of Saint George, while the others chatted, watching his work with interest, for he succeeded well with it.

" I say that if we stay here some time yet, when peace comes we shall be retired."

" Sure enough. I have only four years more to serve, and I have been here six months !"

" That doesn't count for retirement," said another, at the moment when a cannon-ball whizzing over the group struck the earth a yard away from Melnikoff, who was coming towards them in the trench.

" It almost killed Melnikoff !" cried a soldier.

" It won't kill me," replied the former.

" Here, take this cross for your bravery," said the young Jewish soldier, finishing the cross and giving it to him.

" No, brother, here the months count for years without exception. There was an order about it," continued the talker.

" Whatever happens, there will surely be, on the conclusion of peace, a review by the Emperor at Warsaw, and if we are not retired we shall have an unlimited furlough."

Just at this instant a small cannon-ball passing over their heads with a ricochet, seemed to moan and whistle together and fell on a stone.

"Attention!" said one of the soldiers.
" Perhaps between now and night you will
get your definite furlough !"

Everybody began to laugh. Two hours
had not passed, evening had not yet come, before two of them had, in effect, received their
"definite furlough," and five had been wounded, but the rest continued to joke as before.

In the morning the two mortars had been
put in order, and Volodia received at ten
o'clock the order from the commander of
the bastion to assemble his men and go
with them upon the battery. Once at work,
there remained no trace of that terror which
the evening before showed itself so plainly.
Vlang alone did not succeed in overcoming
it ; he hid himself, and bent down every instant. Vassina had also lost his coolness,
he was excited and *saluted.* As to Volodia, stirred by an enthusiastic satisfaction, he
thought no more of the danger. The joy
he felt at doing his duty well, at being no
longer a coward, at feeling himself, on the
contrary, full of courage, the feeling of commanding and the presence of twenty men,
who he knew were watching him with curiosity, had made a real hero of him. Being

even a little vain of his bravery, he got up on the *banquette*, unbuttoning his coat so as to be well observed. The commander of the bastion, in going his rounds, although he had been accustomed during eight months to courage in all its forms, could not help admiring this fine-looking boy with animated face and eyes, his unbuttoned coat exposing a red shirt, which confined a white and delicate neck, clapping his hands, and crying in a voice of command, " First! second!" and jumping gayly on the rampart to see where his shell had fallen. At half-past eleven the firing stopped on both sides, and at noon precisely began the assault on the Malakoff mamelon, as well as upon the second, third, and fifth bastions.

XXIII.

On this side of the bay, between Inkerman and the fortifications of the north, two sailors were standing, in the middle of the day, on Telegraph Height. Near them an officer was looking at Sebastopol through a field-glass, and another on horseback, accompanied by a Cossack, had just rejoined him near the great signal-pole.

The sun soared over the gulf, where the water, covered with ships at anchor, and with sail and row boats in motion, played merrily in its warm and luminous rays. A light breeze, which scarcely shook the leaves of the stunted oak bushes that grew beside the signal-station, filled the sails of the boats, and made the waves ripple softly. On the other side of the gulf Sebastopol was visible, unchanged, with its unfinished church, its column, its quay, the boulevard which cut the hill with a green band, the elegant library building, its little lakes of azure blue, with their forests of masts, its picturesque aqueducts, and, above all that, clouds of a bluish tint, formed by powder-smoke, lighted up from time to time by the red flame of the firing. It was the same proud and beautiful Sebastopol, with its festal air, surrounded on one side by the yellow smoke-crowned hills, on the other by the sea, deep blue in color, and sparkling brilliantly in the sun. At the horizon, where the smoke of a steamer traced a black line, white, narrow clouds were rising, precursors of a wind. Along the whole line of the fortifications, along the heights, especially on the left side, spurted

out suddenly, torn by a visible flash, although
it was broad daylight, plumes of thick white
smoke, which, assuming various forms, extended, rose, and colored the sky with sombre tints.   These jets of smoke came out on
all sides — from the hills, from the hostile
batteries, from the city — and flew towards
the sky.   The noise of the explosions shook
the air with a continuous roar.   Towards
noon these smoke-puffs became rarer and
rarer, and the vibrations of the air strata
became less frequent.

   "Do you know that the second bastion
is no longer replying?" said the hussar officer on horseback; "it is entirely demol-
ished.   It is terrible!"

   "Yes, and the Malakoff replies twice out
of three times," answered the one who was
looking through the field-glass.   "This silence is driving me mad!   They are firing
straight on the Korniloff battery, and that
is not replying."

   "You'll see it will be as I said; towards
noon they will cease firing.   It is always that
way.   Come and take breakfast, they are
waiting for us.   There is nothing more to
see here."

"Wait, don't bother me," replied, with marked agitation, the one looking through the field-glass.

"What is it?—what's the matter?"

"There is a movement in the trenches; they are marching in close columns."

"Yes, I see it well," said one of the sailors; "they are advancing by columns. We must set the signal."

"But see, there—see! They are coming out of the trenches!"

They could see, in fact, with the naked eye black spots going down from the hill into the ravine, and proceeding from the French batteries towards our bastions. In the foreground, in front of the former, black spots could be seen very near our lines. Suddenly, from different points of the bastion at the same time, spurted out the white plumes of the discharges, and, thanks to the wind, the noise of a lively fusillade could be heard, like the patter of a heavy rain against the windows. The black lines advanced, wrapped in a curtain of smoke, and came nearer. The fusillade increased in violence. The smoke burst out at shorter and shorter intervals, extended rapidly along the line in

a single light, lilac-colored cloud, unrolling
and enlarging itself by turns, furrowed here
and there by flashes or rent by black points.
All the noises mingled together in the tu-
mult of one continued roar.

" It is an assault," said the officer, pale
with emotion, handing his glass to the sailor.

Cossacks and officers on horseback went
along the road, preceding the commander-
in-chief in his carriage, accompanied by his
suite. Their faces expressed the painful
emotion of expectation.

" It is impossible that it is taken!" said
the officer on horseback.

" God in heaven!—the flag! Look now!"
cried the other, choked by emotion, turning
away from the glass. " The French flag is
in the Malakoff mamelon!"

" Impossible!"

XXIV.

Koseltzoff the elder, who had had the
time during the night to win and lose again
all his winnings, including even the gold-
pieces sewn in the seams of his uniform,
was sleeping, towards morning, in the barracks of the fifth bastion, a heavy but deep

sleep, when the sinister cry rang out, repeated by different voices, " The alarm !"

" Wake up, Mikhaïl Semenovitch ! It is
an assault !" a voice cried in his ear.

" A school-boy trick," he replied, opening
his eyes without believing the news ; but
when he perceived an officer, pale, agitated,
running wildly from one corner to another,
he understood all, and the thought that he
might perhaps be taken for a coward re-
fusing to join his company in a critical moment, gave him such a violent start that he
rushed out and ran straight to find his soldiers. The cannon were dumb, but the mus-
ket-firing was at its height, and the bullets
were whistling, not singly but in swarms,
just as the flights of little birds pass over
our heads in autumn. The whole of the
place occupied by the battalion the evening
before was filled with smoke, with cries, and
with curses. On his way he met a crowd
of soldiers and wounded, and thirty paces
farther on he saw his company brought to
a stand against a wall.

" The Swartz redoubt is occupied," said
a young officer. " All is lost !"

" What stuff and nonsense !" he angrily

replied, and drawing his small rusty sword
from its scabbard, shouted, " Forward, children !   Hurrah !"

His strong and resounding voice stimu-
lated his own courage, and he ran forward
along the traverse.   Fifty soldiers dashed after him with a shout.   They came out on an
open place, and a hail of bullets met them.
Two struck him simultaneously, but he did
not have time to understand where they had
hit him, or whether they had bruised or had
wounded him, for in the smoke before him
blue uniforms and red trousers started up,
and cries were heard which were not Russian.   A Frenchman sitting on the rampart
was waving his hat and shouting.   The conviction that he would be killed whetted
Koseltzoff's courage.   He continued to run
forward ; some soldiers passed him, others
appeared suddenly from another side and
began to run with him.   The distance between them and the blue uniforms, who re-
gained their intrenchments by running, remained the same, but his feet stumbled
over the dead and the wounded.   Arrived
at the outer ditch, everything became confused before his eyes, and he felt a violent

pain in his chest. A half hour later he was lying on a stretcher near the Nicholas barrack. He knew he was wounded, but he felt no pain. He would have liked, nevertheless, to drink something cold, and to feel himself lying more comfortably.

A stout little doctor with black whiskers came up to him and unbuttoned his overcoat. Koseltzoff looked over his chin at the face of the doctor, who was examining his wound without causing him the least pain. He, having covered the wounded man again with his shirt, wiped his fingers on the lapels of his coat, and turning aside his head, passed to another in silence. Koseltzoff mechanically followed with his eyes all that was going on about him, and remembering the fifth bastion, congratulated himself with great satisfaction. He had valiantly done his duty. It was the first time since he was in the service that he had performed it in a way that he had nothing to reproach himself for. The surgeon, who had just dressed another officer's wound, pointed him out to a priest, who had a fine large red beard, and who stood there with a cross.

" Am I going to die ?" Koseltzoff asked him, seeing him come near.

The priest made no reply, but recited a prayer and held the cross down to him. Death had no terror for Koseltzoff. Carrying the cross to his lips with weakening hands, he wept.

" Are the French driven back ?" he asked the priest in a firm voice.

" Victory is ours along the whole line," answered the latter, hiding the truth to spare the feelings of the dying man, for the French flag was already flying on the Malakoff mamelon.

" Thank God !" murmured the wounded man, whose tears ran down his cheeks unnoticed. The memory of his brother passed through his mind for a second. " God grant him the same happiness !" he said.

XXV.

But such was not Volodia's lot. While he was listening to a tale that Vassina was relating, the alarm cry, " The French are coming !" made his blood rush immediately back to his heart; he felt his cheeks pale and turn cold, and he remained a second

stupefied. Then looking around, he saw the
soldiers button their coats and glide out one
after the other, and he heard one of them,
Melnikoff, probably, say, in a joking way,
" Come, children, let's offer him bread and
salt."

Volodia and Vlang, who did not leave his
heels, went out together and ran to the battery. On one side as well as on the other
the artillery had ceased firing. The despicable and cynical cowardice of the yunker
still more than the coolness of the soldiers
had the effect of restoring his courage.

" Am I like him?" he thought, rushing
quickly towards the parapet, near which the
mortars were placed. From there he distinctly saw the French dash across the space,
free from every obstacle, and run straight
towards him. Their bayonets, sparkling in
the sun, were moving in the nearest trenches. A small, square-shouldered Zouave ran
ahead of the others, sabre in hand, leaping
over the ditches. " Grape!" shouted Volodia, throwing himself down from the parapet. But the soldiers had already thought
of it, and the metallic noise of the grape,
thrown first by one mortar and then by

the other, thundered over his head. "First! second!" he ordered, running across between the two mortars, completely forgetting the danger. Shouts and the musket reports of the battalion charged with the defence of the battery were heard on one side, and suddenly on the left arose a desperate clamor, repeated by many voices: "They are coming in our rear!" and Volodia, turning around, saw a score of Frenchmen. One of them, a fine man with a black beard, ran towards him, and halting ten paces from the battery, fired at him point-blank and went on. Volodia, petrified, could not believe his eyes. In front of him, on the rampart, were blue uniforms, and two Frenchmen who were spiking a cannon. With the exception of Melnikoff, killed by a bullet at his side, and Vlang, who with downcast eyes, and face inflamed by fury, was brandishing a handspike, no one was left.

"Follow me, Vladimir Semenovitch! follow me!" shouted Vlang, in a despairing tone, defending himself with the lever from the French who came behind him. The yunker's menacing look, and the blow which he struck two of them, made them halt.

" Follow me, Vladimir Semenovitch !—
What are you waiting for ?   Fly !" and he
threw himself into the trench, from which
our infantry were firing on the enemy.   He
immediately came out of it, however, to see
what had become of his beloved lieutenant.
A shapeless thing, clothed in a gray overcoat, lay, face to earth, on the spot where Volodia stood, and the whole place was filled by
the French, who were firing at our men.

XXVI.

Vlang found his battery again in the second line of defence, and of the twenty soldiers who recently composed it, only eight
were alive.

Towards nine o'clock in the evening Vlang
and his men were crossing the bay in a steamboat in the direction of Severnaïa.   The boat
was laden with wounded, with cannon, and
with horses.   The firing had stopped everywhere.   The stars sparkled in the sky as on
the night before, but a strong wind was blow-
ing and the sea was rough.   On the first and
second bastions flames flashed up close to the
ground, preceding explosions which shook
the atmosphere and showed stones and black

objects of strange form thrown into the air. Something near the docks was on fire, and a red flame was reflected in the water. The bridge, covered with people, was lighted up by fires from the Nicholas battery. A great sheaf of flames seemed to rise over the water on the distant point of the Alexander battery, and lighted up the under side of a cloud of smoke which hovered over it. As on the preceding evening, the lights of the hostile fleet sparkled afar on the sea, calm and insolent. The masts of our scuttled vessels, slowly settling into the depths of the water, contrasted sharply against the red glow of the fires. On the deck of the steamboat no one spoke. Now and then, in the midst of the regular chopping of the waves struck by the wheels, and the hissing of escaping steam, could be heard the snorting of horses, the striking of their iron-shod hoofs on the planks, the captain speaking a few words of command, and also the dolorous groaning of the wounded. Vlang, who had not eaten since the day before, drew a crust of bread from his pocket and gnawed it, but at the thought of Volodia he broke out sobbing so violently that the soldiers were surprised at it.

"Look! our Vlang is eating bread and weeping," said Vassina.

"Strange!" added one of them.

"See! they have burned our barracks!" he continued, sighing. "How many of our fellows are dead, and dead to no purpose, for the French have got possession!"

"We have scarcely come out alive. We must thank God for it," said Vassina.

"It's all the same. It is maddening!"

"Why? Do you think they will lead a happy life there? Wait a bit; we will take them back. We will still lose some of our men, possibly, but as true as God is holy, if the emperor orders it we will take them back! Do you think they have been left as they were? Come, come; these were only naked walls. The intrenchments were blown up. He has planted his flag on the mamelon, it is true, but he won't risk himself in the town. Wait a bit; we won't be behindhand with you! Only give us time," he said, looking in the direction of the French.

"It will be so, that's sure," said another, with conviction.

On the whole line of the bastions of Sebastopol, where during whole months an ardent and energetic life was stirring, where during months death alone relieved the agony of the heroes, one after the other, who inspired the enemy's terror, hatred, and finally admiration—on these bastions, I say, there was not a single soul, everything there was dead, fierce, frightful, but not silent, for everything all around was falling in with a din. On the earth, torn up by a recent explosion, were lying, here and there, broken beams, crushed bodies of Russians and French, heavy cast-iron cannon overturned into the ditch by a terrible force, half buried in the ground and forever dumb, bomb-shells, balls, splinters of beams, ditches, bomb-proofs, and more corpses, in blue or in gray overcoats, which seemed to have been shaken by supreme convulsions, and which were lighted up now every instant by the red fire of the explosions which resounded in the air.

The enemy well saw that something unusual was going on in formidable Sebastopol, and the explosions, the silence of death on the bastions, made them tremble. Under the impression of the calm and firm resistance of the last day they did not yet dare believe in the disappearance of their invincible adversary, and they awaited, silent and motionless, the end of the dismal night.

The army of Sebastopol, like a sea whose liquid mass, agitated and uneasy, spreads and overflows, moved slowly forward in the dark night, undulating into the impenetrable gloom, over the bridge on the bay, proceeding towards Severnaïa, leaving behind them those spots where so many heroes had fallen, sprinkling them with their blood, those places defended during eleven months against an enemy twice as strong as itself, and which it had received the order this very day to abandon without a fight.

The first impression caused by this order of the day weighed heavily on the heart of every Russian ; next the fear of pursuit was the dominant feeling with all. The soldiers, accustomed to fight in the places they were abandoning, felt themselves without defence the moment they left those behind. Uneasy, they crowded together in masses at the entrance of the bridge, which was lifted by violent wind gusts. Through the obstruction of regiments, of militiamen, of wagons, some crowding the others, the infantry, whose muskets clashed together, and

the officers carrying orders, made a passage
for themselves with difficulty. The inhabitants and the military servants accompanying the baggage begged and wept to be per-
mitted to cross, while the artillery, in a hurry
to go away, rolled along noisily, coming
down towards the bay. Although the attention was distracted by a thousand details,
the feeling of self-preservation, and the desire to fly as soon as possible from that fatal
spot, filled each one's soul. It was thus
with the mortally wounded soldier lying
among five hundred other unfortunates on
the flag-stones of the Paul quay, begging
God for death; with the exhausted militia-
man, who by a last effort forces his way
into the compact crowd to leave a free passage for a superior officer; with the general
who is commanding the passage with a firm
voice, and restraining the impatient soldiers; with the straggling sailor or the battalion on the march, almost stifled by the
moving crowd; with the wounded officer
borne by four soldiers, who, stopped by the
crowd, lay down the stretcher near the
Nicholas barracks; with the old artilleryman, who, during sixteen years, has not left

the cannon which, with the assistance of his comrades and at the command of his chief, incomprehensible for him, he is about to tumble over into the bay; and, at length, with the sailors who have just scuttled their ships, and are vigorously rowing away in their boats.

Arrived at the end of the bridge, each soldier, with very few exceptions, takes off his cap and crosses himself. But besides this feeling he has another, more poignant, deeper—a feeling akin to repentance, to shame, to hatred; for it is with an inexpressible bitterness of heart that each of them sighs, utters threats against the enemy, and, as he reaches the north side, throws a last look upon abandoned Sebastopol.

SELECTED READINGS

Berlin, Isaiah. *The Hedgehog and The Fox*. Mentor Book, 1957.
—— "Tolstoy and the Enlightenment," *Encounter*, February, 1961.

Fausset, Hugh l'Anson. *Tolstoy: the Inner Drama*. London, 1927.

Gorki, Maxim. *Reminiscences of Tolstoy, Chekhov and Andreyev*. New York, 1959.

Hofmann, Modeste, and André Pierre. *By Deeds of Truth: The Life of Leo Tolstoy*. Tr. by Ruth Whipple Fermand. New York, 1958.

Howells, William Dean. *My Literary Passions*. New York, 1895.

Kuzminskaya (Behrs), T. A. *Tolstoy As I Knew Him*. New York, 1948.

Lavrin, Janko. *Tolstoy, an Approach*. London, 1948.

Leon, Derrick. *Tolstoy, His Life and Work*. London, 1946.

Lukacs, Georg. *Studies in Modern European Realism*. London, 1950.

Mann, Thomas. *Three Essays*. Tr. by H. T. Lowe-Porter. New York, 1959.

Maude, Aylmer. *The Life of Tolstoy*. New York, 1953.

Merejkowski, Dmitri. *Tolstoy As Man and Artist, With an Essay on Dostoevsky*. New York, 1902.

Noyes, George R. *Tolstoy*. New York, 1918.

Redpath, Theodore. *Tolstoy*. London, 1960.

Rolland, Romain. *Tolstoy*. New York, 1911.

Simmons, Ernest J. *Leo Tolstoy*. Boston, 1946.

Steiner, George. *Tolstoy or Dostoevsky?* New York, 1959.

Suares, André. *Trois grands vivants*. Paris, 1937.

Tolstoi, Alexandra. *A Life of My Father*. Tr. by Elizabeth R. Hapgood. New York, 1953.

The Countess of Tolstoy's Later Diary. Tr. by Alexander Werth. New York, 1929.

The Diary of Tolstoy's Wife. Tr. by Alexander Werth. New York, 1929.

Family Views of Tolstoy. Tr. by Louise and Aylmer Maude. London, 1926.

The Private Diary of Leo Tolstoy. Tr. by Louise and Aylmer Maude. New York, 1927.

Tolstoi, Leon L. *The Truth About My Father*. New York, 1924.

Zweig, Stefan. *Adepts in Self-Portraiture: Casanova, Stendhal, Tolstoy*. Tr. by Eden and Cedar Paul. London, 1930.

ANN ARBOR PAPERBACKS *reissues of works of enduring merit*

The University of Michigan Press   *Ann Arbor*